"What kind of man... interests you?"

"The kind who remembers—" Kate snapped her lips shut before the rest of that sentence could see daylight.

Gabe moved even closer. "The kind of man who remembers...what?"

"Nothing." She pretended preoccupation with counting the people in line in front of them.

"There's no need to get so upset just because I can't remember kissing you."

Kate opened her mouth to refute that, but nothing came out, and she ended up staring at him for a minute. "That has nothing to do with this," she finally said.

"I think it does. I think that's what all of this is about."

"Well, it isn't," she snapped. "I'm sorry I ever even told you about that. Forget it."

Gabe put his lips so close to her ear, he almost singed them on her furious blush. "Kissing you is all I can think about."

Dear Reader,

Each year, I tell my family and friends that *this* Christmas is the best one ever. And each year, it really is! I love everything about Christmas—the busyness of the season, the colors, the lights, the smells, the music, the food, the gifts, the giving and the movies. It wouldn't be December if I couldn't warm my feet and backside in front of the fireplace and warm my heart and soul with the magic of *Miracle On 34th Street*. Of all the wonderful old movies, this classic story of love, hope and faith triumphing over cynicism is my all-time favorite. In the film, a very young Natalie Wood plays the role of Sharon, and her mother, Doris, is played by the beautiful Maureen O'Hara. Their lives are touched by a man named Kris Kringle and they each learn that believing in Santa Claus requires a commitment of the heart. The story has a happily-ever-after ending which, in my opinion, is the only kind of ending any story should have. Is it any wonder, then, that I would one day write a Christmas romance with the same theme as my favorite movie? My family would say the wonder is that I didn't write it sooner!

One of the Christmas traditions at our house is movie night. We reserve one evening before the official holiday to have dinner as a family and watch whatever movies I choose. (I'm the mother; that's why I get to choose the movies. And you guessed it, *Miracle On 34th Street* always makes the cut, along with *A Christmas Story* and whatever other movies appeal to me when I'm at the video store.) Attendance is required, and although they'd never admit it, I believe the kids love the tradition and the movies as much as I do. After all, it wouldn't be the best Christmas ever without a dusting of hope, faith, romance—and Santa Claus!

Happy Holidays!

Karen Toller Whittenburg

Karen Toller Whittenburg

THE SANTA SUIT

Harlequin Books

TORONTO • NEW YORK • LONDON
AMSTERDAM • PARIS • SYDNEY • HAMBURG
STOCKHOLM • ATHENS • TOKYO • MILAN
MADRID • WARSAW • BUDAPEST • AUCKLAND

For Santa and the elves—
because I believe

ISBN 0-373-16708-3

THE SANTA SUIT

Copyright © 1997 by Karen Whittenburg Crane.

Prologue

"Is too!"

"Is not!"

From the sidelines, seven-year-old Andy Harmon watched the debate between his twin sister, Abby, and an upperclassman... a second-grader named Isabelle. It was clear this was an argument Abby couldn't win, no matter how loud she got, and he wished she hadn't started it.

"There's no such thing as Santa Claus." Abby flicked one of her copper-colored braids behind her shoulder. "My mother told me and she never lies. Does she, Andy?"

He didn't want to answer. Not with Tyler, his best friend, standing right next to him. How could he say there wasn't a Santa, when he knew Tyler believed there was? But if he called Mom a liar, Abby would get him in trouble, for sure. He glared at his sister, who glared right back. "It's almost time for the bell," he said, stalling. "And I'm not wasting any more of my recess. Let's go play, Tyler."

"*You* believe in Santa, don't you, Andy?" Isabelle's soft question stopped him in his tracks, and her smile kept him there. She had long blond curls and pretty blue eyes and she could outrun every boy in second grade, plus a bunch of the third-graders. And right now, more than anything, Andy wished there was a Santa, just so that he could tell Isabelle he believed. But there wasn't. Mom had said.

"No," he said sadly. "I don't."

Abby beamed. "I told you so."

Isabelle looked startled and terribly concerned. "But you have to believe in Santa," she said. "Or you won't get any presents."

Abby put her hands on her hips. "We get lots of presents, don't we, Andy? But not from Santa Claus, because he's just a made-up person!"

"He is not made-up." Isabelle smugly put her hands on her hips. "I get presents from him every year."

"No, you don't," Abby insisted. "Your mom buys all the stuff and just pretends it's from Santa Claus."

Isabelle rolled her eyes. "Oh, she does not!"

"She does, too," Abby insisted. "Ask her."

"I'll ask my *daddy*. He knows everything about Santa Claus and how come the reindeer can fly and the names of all the elves in the toy shop, too." Isabelle reclaimed her upperclassman superiority with a shrug. "But *you* don't have a daddy to ask, so how could you know?"

"Shut up, Issy!" Andy stepped closer to Abby, bringing them shoulder to shoulder. "We don't want a dumb old daddy, who thinks elves make toys and reindeer can fly. That's just more lies!"

"Yeah," Abby added her support. "Who wants a big, fat liar for a daddy?"

"Well, your mom's a big, fat, *stupid* liar!"

"She is not!" Abby's hands balled into fists. "Take that back, Issy!"

Isabelle shook her head. "She's a liar and she must be really stupid not to believe in Santa Claus."

Tyler elbowed his way between the girls. "My granddad told me you have to believe in Santa when you're a little kid or you can't when you're a grown-up. Maybe their mom just didn't know about Santa until it was too late."

The truth hung there in the crisp morning air, and Andy felt it all over, like a big hug. What if Santa *was* real and Mom just didn't know it?

"That's *so* dumb." Issy wrinkled her nose in disdain and pushed Tyler out of the way. "You can believe any time you want to," she said to Abby. "Your mom was stupid when she was a little kid and she's still stupid. If she wasn't, she'd know Santa's a real person."

"She's *not* stupid!" Abby yelled in frustration.

"Yes, she is," Issy said smugly.

"She is not!"

"Yes, she is, yes, she is, yes, she is, yes, she is." Isabelle ran the words together in a mocking sing-song, until Abby's eyes glistened with angry tears, until she made one last, tear-choked protest. "She is not."

"Oh, don't be such a crybaby." With a toss of her long, gold curls, Isabelle started to walk away, the winner.

So Andy tripped her.

LATELY, Katherine had been spending a good deal of time reflecting on her decision to become a single mom. It had seemed like such a great idea. All the joys of parenthood, none of the hassles of a relationship. But now, sitting in the office of a stern-faced Sister Mary Cornelia, Katherine had to wonder what in hell she'd been thinking. For all the trouble a man would create in her life, there were moments...this one being a prime example...when she wished there was someone who was obligated to sit beside her.

"If this was the first time an incident such as this had occurred," Sister Mary Cornelia was saying, "I'd be more understanding. But your children are quite precocious, Mrs. Harmon, and they...."

"*Miss* Harmon," Katherine corrected politely.

Sister acknowledged the interruption with a tart smile. "Your children do speak their minds."

"I encourage them to have opinions," Katherine said proudly.

"Oh, yes. Everyone here at Saint Julian's is well aware of Abigail's and Andrew's opinions on a variety of topics. And while we do promote independent thinking and encourage discussion, slugging it out in the play yard cannot be considered a fair exchange of ideas."

Katherine sighed. "What was it this time? The stork versus the sperm bank again?"

Sister Mary Cornelia shuddered, sending a faint ripple through the folds of her black habit. "Thankfully, *that* subject hasn't been mentioned again. This latest fracas seems to have been caused by a disagreement over Saint Nicholas.''

That was bad news. "Abby and Andy were fighting over a saint?''

"Saint Nick," Sister explained patiently. "Santa Claus.''

"Oh, that Saint Nick." Katherine relaxed, feeling suddenly more hopeful that her children weren't about to be expelled from Saint Julian's hallowed halls. "Well, at least they didn't pick a fight over a really important saint. Saint Peter, for instance. Or the Blessed Virgin.''

Sister's pinched lips puckered anew. "There are always reasons to count our blessings, Mrs. Harmon." Pressing her palms together as if she were about to pray, she observed Katherine for a moment. "At this season of the year, we do our best to emphasize the true meaning of Christmas. But the children are young and imaginative, and it's unrealistic to think we can forbid any mention of Santa Claus.''

"You should forbid it, anyway," Katherine stated flatly. "Santa Claus is your basic flat-out whopper. Andy and Abby can't be faulted for refusing to believe it.''

Sister Mary Cornelia folded her hands on the desktop and leaned forward. "Life at Saint Julian's would be much less eventful if you didn't insist on such strict standards of truth for Abigail and Andrew.''

"I believe in giving my children straightforward, honest answers," Katherine said firmly. "And I won't apologize for it.''

"I'm not suggesting you should. However, when

they're at school, I insist they demonstrate compassion and tolerance for the truth as others perceive it."

Katherine was roused to the defense of the twins' First Amendment rights. "Are you saying Abby and Andy have no right to state their opinion in a public place? Regardless of who does or doesn't agree with them?"

Sister Mary Cornelia didn't even blink. "This is a private school, Mrs. Harmon, and I'm personally responsible for supervising the behavior of several hundred students. I don't necessarily share the opinions of every parent who sits where you're sitting now, although in this instance, I do happen to agree with you. However, I would rather bungee-jump off the Empire State Building than face a classroom full of parents whose children have been disabused of their belief in Santa Claus because of your twins' inalienable right to speak their minds."

Katherine couldn't believe her ears. "You expect me to tell my children it's okay to lie, as long as they're only talking about a big fat guy in red velvet?"

"I expect them...and you...to keep an open mind on the subject."

Indignant words tumbled into one another on her tongue, but Katherine battled them back. Saint Julian's was the best preparatory school in New York, the booster rocket to an education of unlimited prestige and opportunity. She wasn't going to ruin her children's lives over something as silly as Santa Claus. After all, she'd had to caution them about discussing sex in a first-grade open forum. Was this really all that different? "I'm not sure I can keep an open mind about Santa Claus, but I assure you the twins won't be involved in any more fights on the subject."

"You're always most cooperative, Mrs. Harmon." Sister Mary Cornelia stood, leaving Katherine to wonder how anyone with such ruler-straight posture could sit in the first place. "As a peacekeeping measure, however, I'm giving your twins a little extra holiday time. You may take them home with you when you leave."

Katherine froze with her coat sleeves halfway up her arms. "You're suspending them from school for not believing in Santa Claus?"

"No, indeed." Sister Mary Cornelia walked to the door and opened it. "I certainly don't want *my* name on Santa's naughty list this close to Christmas."

"Very funny." Katherine shrugged on her coat and slung the strap of her handbag across her shoulder. "It isn't nice to kid around about suspending children from school, you know."

"Oh, I wasn't kidding, Mrs. Harmon. There are only three more days of school before semester break, anyway, and I'm sure the time spent with you will be much more beneficial to Andrew and Abigail than any busywork the teacher might contrive for them between now and Friday."

"But I have to work," Katherine protested, her mind racing through the next seventy-two hours, making lists of all the things she had to do, counting up all the obstacles in her path, even before she factored in the demands of two seven-year-olds. "The day care can't take them until next week, and Mrs. Cassidy, our housekeeper, left last night to spend the holidays with her family in Oregon and..." Panic simmered inside her and came out in a plea. "You *can't* suspend them now."

Sister Mary Cornelia patted Katherine's shoulder. "Think of it as three extra days to enjoy long, truthful discussions with your children on a variety of subjects."

Katherine buttoned her coat, wishing she hadn't worked so hard to get the twins admitted to Saint Julian's in the first place. "And all this time, Sister, I thought you lacked a sense of humor."

"Just because I dress solemnly, doesn't mean I make solemnity a habit, Mrs. Harmon."

"Miss," Katherine corrected, losing all patience with wisecracking nuns. "*Miss* Harmon, not Mrs."

"Yes, of course. I'm sorry. I do keep trying to assign the twins a father, don't I?" Sister Mary Cornelia smiled easily. "I suppose it stems from my belief that children need both a mother *and* a father."

"My children need a father about as much as they need three extra days out of school." Pulling on her gloves, Katherine snapped the leather against her wrist as she stepped through the doorway into the outer office. "And for the record, Abby and Andy *do* have a father. I just don't know exactly who he is."

Sister Mary Cornelia closed the door in a distinctly humorless and peremptory manner, leaving Katherine pleased to have gotten the last word on at least one subject. Then, with a resigned, but frustrated sigh, she prepared to retrieve her mouthy children.

"WE DON'T HAVE to go to school anymore?" Abby asked for the hundredth time, clearly delighted by the prospect. "Are we gratuated?"

"Don't be dumb," Andy told her.

"I'm smarter'n you," she replied.

"You're not neither."

"Either," Katherine corrected automatically as she directed the twins into the ancient elevator in the Fitzpatrick Building and pushed the button for the twelfth-floor offices of *Contemporary Woman* magazine. "You'll both go back to school after the holidays. Now, remember what I told you, I expect exemplary behavior this afternoon. I have a very important deadline, and I don't want to hear so much as a peep out of either one of you. Understand?"

"Yes, Mom," they answered, more or less in unison, before Andy nudged his sister with an elbow and Abby reciprocated with a halfhearted punch.

"No more fighting," Katherine said sternly. "You've already lost television privileges for a month. Let's not make it two."

"Okay, Mom." Another unison of sorts, accompanied by a slightly more subtle poke and return punch.

Katherine tapped her toe impatiently, weary even before she could reach the stack of work on her desk. Glancing at the slowly ascending numbers on the door panel, she wondered if a bribe would help ensure the twins' cooperation. "Tell you what...if you're extra good this afternoon, we'll do something fun tomorrow.''

Andy looked interested. ''Will you take us to the Jekyll and Hyde restaurant?''

''No, Andy!'' Abby answered first in a good, if higher-pitched, imitation of Katherine's voice. ''Mom, we can't go there. You have to cross a bridge that moves and monsters jump out and everybody screams. Emily went there with her brother and she was scared silly. She told me.''

''Oh, yeah,'' Andy sneered. ''Well, Tyler went and he said it was way cool! Besides, I wouldn't be scared. I'd leap over the bridge and into the restaurant and melt the monsters with my laser gun.'' He jumped and landed in a fighting stance, legs braced, elbows jutting, eyes narrowed to slits of suspicion. *''Zeeeep! Zeeeep, zeeeep! Zeeeep!''* The imaginary laser gun fired repeatedly, until Katherine reached down and turned it back into a normal little-boy hand. Andy looked up at her, pleading. ''I'll protect you and Abby. Please, can we go there? Please?''

''You may go there when you're thirty-five,'' Katherine told him. ''Not a moment before.''

''But, Mom...'' Andy's protest had barely begun when Abby cut him off. ''I told you so.''

Andy would have elbowed her again, but Katherine separated them. ''We'll visit the library,'' she said. ''Or one of the museums.''

''Whee...'' Andy muttered under his breath, but Katherine ignored him and Abby's sullen expression. Okay, so she was better at editing magazines than at creating fun learning experiences for her kids. But she was a damn good mother, and these two adorable hoodlums should be thanking their lucky stars they had her.

"How about a carriage ride in Central Park?" she offered as a compromise.

"Ice-skating," Abby countered.

"Jekyll and Hyde," Andy insisted stubbornly.

Reluctantly Katherine topped them both. "FAO Schwarz."

"Really?"

"You mean it?"

Katherine nodded. "You may each buy one toy for yourself and one to give to someone less fortunate."

"Yes! Cool! I'm buying Jet Jupiter, Laser Ranger!" The laser gun fired again. *"Zeeeep! Zeeeep!"*

Abby wrinkled her nose to show her superior taste in toys. "I want Bookworm Barbie. She comes with glasses and her own bookstore."

Barbie in bifocals. "Wonderful," Katherine said.

"Zeeeep! Zeeeep! Jet Jupiter blasts Bookworm Barbie into orbit!"

"You better keep your stupid toy away from my Barbie doll, Andy!"

Katherine had never been so glad to reach her floor. They weren't even inside her office yet, and already she'd used up her best bribe and her last aspirin. When the elevator doors finally lumbered apart, she grasped each child by the hand and led them firmly to the receptionist's desk. Janeen looked up, her expression changing from surprise to pleasure in an instant. "Hiya, kiddies," she said with a smile. "Why aren't you in school today?"

"We got kicked out," Abby informed her brightly. "We're dink-quints."

"Delinquents," Katherine interpreted as she sorted through a sizable stack of message slips.

"Uh-oh," Janeen said, her voice smiling even though she wasn't. "It isn't good to be delinquents this close to Christmas. What's Santa Claus going to think?"

Katherine tossed the phone slips onto the desk with a severe frown. "Santa Claus *doesn't* think, because he isn't real. Abby and Andy know that."

Janeen looked shocked. "Santa's not *real?*"

Andy looked at her, hopefully. "Do you believe in Santa Claus?"

"Well, of course." Janeen lowered her aesthetically perfect eyebrows in Katherine's direction. "Only an old Scrooge doesn't believe in Santa Claus."

"Don't encourage them, please." Katherine planted a hand on each of the twin red heads and tipped them up to look at her. "Janeen doesn't believe in Santa Claus. No one over the age of eight believes in Santa Claus. And that's the truth." With a scowl for her receptionist, she urged the children toward her office.

"I do, too, believe," Janeen called after them. "I do believe in Santa."

ANDY DUMPED the box of crayons on the table and scattered them, looking for green. He glanced over at Abby to see if she had it, but she was huddled over a yellow pad of paper, drawing carefully with the red crayon. "What're you drawin'?" he asked. "I'm drawing a monster with slime comin' out his nose."

"That's gross," she said without looking up.

He tried to see what she was drawing, but she kept her arm around the pad, so he couldn't. She was probably just drawing the same old thing she always drew...a house with a dog, a cat, a mom and two kids. But he wanted to talk to her about Santa Claus, and now, while nobody was paying them any attention, was the perfect time. "I've been thinking," he said, letting the words rush toward Abby. "What if the kids at school are right? What if Mom never knew about Santa Claus, when she was a kid? What if he *is* real and she just doesn't know?"

Abby looked at him across the table. "You think Mom is a liar?"

He wiggled uncomfortably. "It wouldn't be a lie if she didn't know."

"She says the reindeer and the elves and the North Pole are all just made-up. They're not real."

"I know she says that, Abby, but what if she just doesn't know? Janeen believes in Santa Claus. What if she's right and Mom's wrong?"

Abby looked at her drawing, then turned it around to show Andy. "I was trying to write a letter to Santa, but I couldn't spell all the words, so I'm drawing a picture of what I want for Christmas."

Andy stared at the drawing, feeling that funny feeling that happened when he and Abby started thinking the same thing at the same time. She'd drawn a house with a dog, a cat, a mom and two kids...only there was a fat man in a red suit standing on the roof, and reindeer flying in the sky, and a lot of trees, and a bunch of other stuff. Andy pointed to a brown blob. "What's that?"

"A turkey."

"You want a turkey for Christmas?"

"I want a turkey dinner on Christmas," she clarified. "I don't want to eat spaghetti at a restaurant like we did last year. I want Mom to cook."

Andy wasn't sure even Santa could make *that* happen. He pointed at something else. "What's that?"

"A real pond, so we can ice-skate. And that's the forest, with real Christmas trees growing in it. And those are decorations for the tree." Her finger moved faster across the paper. "And those are the cookies Mom and I baked for Santa. And that's a real dog and a real cat and the house is yellow like that one in the magazine, and Mom's happy and the cat is purring, and it's a real Christmas." She bit her lower lip. "That's what I want. If Santa's real, he can give me everything in the picture. Can't he, Andy?"

Andy picked up a crayon—the blue one—and drew in another stick figure. "There," he said, angling the pad toward Abby. "That's our dad. If Santa is really real, then he can bring us a daddy, too."

"I don't think Mom will let us keep him."

Andy nodded, certain she was right. "For a week, then. One week with a daddy and all the stuff in the picture. Santa has to be able to do that...if he's real."

Abby took back the drawing and studied it with a

frown. "But how do we find out, Andy? How do we find Santa Claus?"

"I got an idea," he said. "I got a good idea." He leaned closer to Abby, so excited he could barely whisper. "We'll hire a *detective!* They find stuff all the time."

Abby frowned. "But we don't know any detectives."

"Mom does. I heard her talking about him one day on the phone. She said he was just a gory-fried house detective and she said he found the person she was lookin' for and she said that's what everyone in the building pays the Jack Kass to do, anyway."

"Is that his name? Jack Kass?"

"Nah. I think it's another word for detective. But, see, Abby, if everyone in the building pays him to look for people, he must work here somewhere. So it'll be easy to find him." Andy's mind raced with possibilities as he jumped up from the table. "Come on. Janeen will help us."

Abby was slower getting to her feet. "You don't think she'll tell Mom, do you? If Mom finds out, she's gonna be awful mad."

"She won't find out, Abby," he told her confidently. "Not until the detective shows her the real Santa. Then she can't be mad. She'll be too happy."

Abby tore her Christmas picture from the pad, folded it into careful fourths and tucked it into her pocket. "Santa better be real," she said. "Or I'm gonna be mad."

"He's real." Andy was already planning all the

things he wanted to do once Santa brought him a daddy. "He's real, all right, and this is gonna be the best Christmas ever!"

Chapter One

"Tim Wiltham wants to talk to you about the IDS system. Carl needs five minutes to discuss a personnel matter. Gina Haring requested thirty minutes to go over the in-house newsletter. You have reservations at La Bernadin at seven-thirty, a chamber reception, also at seven-thirty, tickets for tonight's Knicks game at eight, and your four-o'clock appointment is waiting in your office."

Gabe Housley stopped shuffling papers to glance at his assistant, Louisa, who matched him stride for stride as he walked down the hallway toward his office. "I don't remember seeing a four-o'clock on my calendar."

"I made the appointment while you were out." Louisa's smiles were rare, so when there was even a trace of one—as there was now—Gabe was instantly alert.

"Who is it?" he asked warily. "Not another of Dad's *clients* who wants to murder him and sue me, is it?"

"I screen your appointments very carefully," she said, as if that were all he needed to know. Louisa

Feigle had managed the day-to-day operations of Housley Security since time began, and she did so with such efficient authority that Gabe was either completely in awe or completely annoyed. Sometimes he was hard-pressed to tell which. She checked her steno pad again. "Your father left word he's on a stakeout and won't be home for dinner."

Gabe rubbed the back of his neck. "I don't suppose he gave you any idea of where he is or what he's investigating this week?"

"Mr. Gunther never reveals the details of his cases. You know that."

"Dad doesn't have cases, Louisa. He has episodes. One week, 'Spenser for Hire.' The next, 'Columbo.'" Gabe paused outside the door of his office. "Tell me again why I let my father wander the streets of New York, pretending to be James Bond?"

"Because he's of legal age, sound mind, and it keeps him out of the office."

"I knew there was a good reason." Gabe passed the sheaf of reports into Louisa's capable hands. "I'll call Tim and Carl. Schedule Gina sometime tomorrow. Phone my regrets on the reception. Cancel the dinner reservations. Leave the basketball tickets in your desk drawer, and I'll pick them up on my way out this evening. If the police chief calls again about Dad's license—"

"You're unavailable." Louisa jotted a note on her pad, as if she might forget…which was about as likely as Gun ever applying for a P.I. license. "Anything else?"

"Call the deli and have them send over a couple

of tuna salad sandwiches around six. On second thought, bring the basketball tickets to me before you leave. I don't want Dad to get his hands on them this time.''

"He said he wouldn't be in the office for days.''

"I'm not taking any chances. The old coot has a sixth sense when it comes to my Knicks tickets. Sometimes I think he has an informant at the box office." Gabe reached for the doorknob. "Now, who did you say is waiting in my office?"

To his dismay, Louisa's stern mouth curved with unmistakable humor. "The Harmons," she said. "Brother and sister. Short. Serious. Anxious to see you.''

"If this turns out to be another elderly couple who wants a bodyguard for their aging Pekinese, I'm giving you the assignment.''

Louisa's sudden and surprising laughter struck fear in his heart, but Gabe bravely entered his office. Two tall leather chairs faced his desk and away from him, and as he closed the door behind him, two strawberry-blond heads popped up over the red leather...one head rising above each hobnailed chairback. "Hi," one said. A girl. He could tell by the Pippi Longstocking braids.

"Hi," said the other. A boy, if one could trust the boyish cowlick and absence of pigtails.

"Hi," Gabe responded, wondering if he could afford to fire Louisa for letting these kids into his office. "Your name wouldn't be Harmon, by any chance, would it?"

The cowlick nodded enthusiastically. "I'm Andy."

"I'm Abby. We're twins," Pigtails confirmed. "We're looking for a Jack Kass. Are you one?"

Gabe ignored the impulse to open the door and yell for Louisa. Instead, he strolled around the chairs and stood behind his desk, eyeing the two rug rats who'd breached his own unwritten rule of security...no kids. Not in his office. Not in his life. But here they were, a boy and a girl, redheads, both of them, with matching blue eyes and a scattering of freckles across their noses. They were twins and they were trouble. Looking for a *jackass,* were they? Well, he'd put the fear of God into them and then he'd find out who put them up to this little prank. Placing his hands on the desktop, he leaned forward, trying to look as intimidating as possible.

"Why aren't you in school?" he asked gruffly.

"It's four." The girl, Abby, didn't seem intimidated. "School's over at three. Don't you know?"

"I haven't been to school in a while."

"Don't you have kids?"

"No." The word popped out, fast and firm. "I'm not married."

Abby eyed him curiously from the depths of the red leather chair. "Our mom's not married and she got us."

"Some people are just lucky, I guess." Gabe shifted his weight, wondering how his intimidation skills had gotten so rusty. "Where *is* your mother?"

"Upstairs." Andy patted the chair arms and explored the room with an inquisitive gaze. "Where's *your* mother?"

"My mother is..." He wondered if he could say 'dead.' It might frighten them. They might start screaming...or crying. Better to avoid that possibility, altogether, he decided, and settled for a vague "I don't have a mother."

"We don't have a daddy," Abby informed him matter-of-factly. "Mom says daddies are redumbbant and we don't need one."

Gabe hadn't a clue as to what that meant, other than that their mother must be a really cold fish. And an irresponsible cold fish, to boot. "Does your mother know where you are?"

"You can call her Mom." Andy smiled, displaying a gap the size of two missing front teeth. "That's what we call her."

"Sometimes we call her Kate the Great." Abby intercepted a stern glance from her brother and made a face at him before she turned a quite beguiling smile on Gabe. "But that's a secret, so you can't tell her."

Kate Harmon. Gabe fitted the names together and had a vague sense of it being familiar, although it didn't trigger any real recognition. "Don't you think you'd better leave, before she comes looking for you?"

"She won't," Abby assured him. "She's busy."

"I'm a little busy, myself," Gabe said sharply. "So why don't you two run along and play a joke on someone else?"

The twins exchanged glances, and then Andy slid

from the chair and stepped up to the desk. "It's not a joke," he said solemnly. "We want to hire you."

"We have to find somebody who's a real person." Abby seconded the motion. "That's why we need a Jack Kass."

Gabe frowned. "*What* did you say?"

"We need a Jack Kass," Abby repeated, looking at him strangely. "You know, a detective."

"A detective? You think a detective is the same as a jackass?"

"That's what Mom said." Andy reached across the desk, picked up a pencil sharpener shaped like a Colt .45 and aimed it at the window. "I heard her. She said a gory-fried house detective finds things because that's what everybody pays the Jack Kass to do. We asked Janeen and she told us you're the house detective, so we came to hire you."

Gabe jerked the pencil sharpener from Andy's lethal fingers and put it back on the desk. Then he sank into his big black chair and observed the redheads, wishing they were a nice, simple older couple with an arthritic Pekinese. "Look, kids," he said. "This is a security company. We install and monitor alarm systems. We provide bodyguards and security personnel. We do electronic data searches and investigative reports. But we don't do detective work and we don't find missing persons."

There was a brief consultation of glances. "We have money." Andy clutched the edge of the desk and leaned forward with a somber man-of-the-world air. "We didn't expect you to do it for nothin'."

"We have our own checkbook." Abby offered that information with a smug toss of braids.

Gabe knew next to nothing about kids, but he was damned impressed to discover that they arrived with their own bank accounts. "You can write checks?"

"Yessss..." Abby stretched the word as if she found the question silly. "Can't you?"

"I deal in cash," Gabe said, just to be disagreeable.

Andy disappeared below the edge of the desk, and when he bobbed up again, he was holding a handful of bills. He opened his hand over the desk and the money fell in crumpled ones. Three of them. A fourth stuck to his fingers, and he had to shake it loose, causing Gabe to wonder where the kid kept his cash. Not that he actually wanted to know.

Andy looked expectantly at Gabe. "Is that enough?"

Gabe fought the impulse to tell the boy to stuff the dollars back in his pocket and looked at Abby, instead. "Where's your money?" he asked.

"I only have one dollar," she said with a pout. "You don't need it, do you?"

Just like a female, Gabe thought. The little twerp was going to let her brother use all of his cash without ever once volunteering to add hers. "You're in luck," Gabe said in his best businesslike tone. "Five dollars is my consultation fee."

Andy looked over his shoulder at Abby, who rolled her eyes, sighed, and bent forward to pull a folded dollar bill out of her sock. "Here." She handed the money to Andy. "But you better make sure Santa pays me back."

"He will." Andy happily added it to the other four. "Five," he said. "Now you're hired."

Gabe hadn't meant to *be* hired. He'd meant to get these kids out of his office. "It isn't quite that easy. Your mother's going to have to give her permission."

Both freckled faces looked horrified by the prospect. "We can't tell her we came to your office," Abby said. "We'd get in a lot of trouble."

"Well, I could get in a lot of trouble, too." Which was true, Gabe realized as he said it. "You should just take your money and forget about hiring a detective until you're older."

The two red heads shook vigorously, in an emphatic dual denial. "We're going to be eight on our birthday," Abby blurted out. "And then it'll be too late."

"Too late for what?"

"To believe in Santa Claus," the boy said seriously. "Do *you* believe Santa is a real person?"

Gabe closed his eyes. *I had to ask,* he thought, then cleared his throat and dredged up his best diplomatic tone of voice. "What I believe isn't important. It's what *you* believe that counts."

Andy was having none of that. "It is, too, important," he insisted. "Me and Abby have to know. Do you believe in Santa Claus?"

Gabe decided he would fire Louisa for this...right after he strangled her. "Well, of course!" he lied with a boisterous laugh. "Doesn't everyone?"

Abby shook her head. "Our Mom doesn't. She says nobody older'n eight believes in Santa."

"She says Santa's a myth." The string of *s* sounds lisped through the gap in Andy's teeth. "She says he's just a made-up story. She says we don't need Santa to have a nice Christmas."

Abby nodded concurrence. "She says we don't need a daddy, either."

He was in over his head here, Gabe realized belatedly. But he'd be damned if he was going to tell these two fatherless kids they didn't need a dad, let alone that there wasn't a Santa Claus. Let their mother be the Grinch. She was obviously a bitter wrinkled-up old crone who sapped all the wonder out of Christmas and begrudged her children the magic of fantasy. Plus, she'd had the gall to call him a jackass when he couldn't even recall who she was. "Your mother's wrong," he stated firmly, sitting straighter in his chair. "Santa Claus is as real as you are."

"He is?"

"He is?"

Their voices were out of sync, but their desire for reassurance was unanimous. Gabe nodded. "He's real."

Andy and Abby grinned at each other, then beamed their delight on Gabe. "Do you know how reindeer fly?" Andy asked, his eager tone revealing that this, too, was an important question.

Gabe barely hesitated. If he was going to get hanged for a liar, he wanted the lies to be his best. "Special hay," he answered. "It's very rare. Only grows in the Alps, and there's only enough to feed eight reindeer for one day every year. Oops. Did I say *eight* reindeer? I meant to say ten. I forgot about Rudolph, and he eats enough for two.''

The twins traded excited glances, and then Abby nailed him with a candid ''What do you know about the elves?''

''Let's see...'' Gabe searched his memory for any and all elf info. ''They're usually short, but that isn't a requirement. They usually have pointed ears, although that's not always true, either. They wear a lot of green. They have funny-looking hats and...shoes with bells on the toes.'' Feeling pleased with those imaginative little details, he checked the twins' expressions and realized they were expecting something more. ''Hmm...'' he said. ''What else could you want to know about Santa's elves?''

''Their names,'' Andy supplied readily. ''We want to know their names.''

''Uh, sure.'' Gabe didn't have any idea whether elves even had names. ''Um... Dancer, Prancer, Donner and Blitzen....''

''Those are the reindeer,'' Abby informed him with a frown. ''Everybody knows that.''

Gabe thumped his forehead with the palm of his hand and won an engaging pair of giggles for his trouble. ''You're absolutely right, Abby. What was I thinking? The elves are named...um...well, there's Doc and Spock, they're the oldest. Then there's Eeeney, Meeney, Miney, and Moe. Buttons and Bo. Curly, Larry and Joe. Sally, Jessie, Raphael, Jerry, and Montel. Oprah, Dave, Jay and Rosie....'' He ran out of talk-show hosts and inspiration. "I'd better stop there, because I'm bound to leave one out, and you know how sensitive elves can be."

Abby nodded, as if she were well acquainted with the idiosyncrasies of the world's elf population. Andy scooted back in the red leather chair and ran his hands back and forth over the wooden arms in a brisk, energetic rhythm, while his legs and feet moved together and apart, together and apart, in an alternate cadence. "So how long will it take you to find him?" he asked.

Gabe was mesmerized by the abundant energy and sheer coordination going on in the red chairs. He'd once been able to rub his stomach and pat his head at the same time, but he hadn't tried it in years. "Find who?"

"Santa Claus," came the rather impatient answer. "We've only got a few more days before it's..."

"Before it's too late. I remember." Gabe stroked his thumb across his jaw. He should never have let these kids start talking. Now, they not only thought he'd agreed to work for them, they expected him to *find* Santa. As if Santa Claus were missing. As if there weren't one on every street corner in the city at this time of year. "Look, kiddos, I can't take your money under false pretenses. You can find the fat guy without my help."

"Where?" Abby asked with sharp suspicion.

"Well, have you tried Macy's? I hear he hangs out there right up through Christmas Eve."

"We don't go to Macy's." Abby's black patent shoes made a continuing *thud-thud, thud-thud,*

thud-thud against the leather chair seat. "Mom doesn't shop there."

"And she wouldn't take us to see Santa in a million years no matter where he was." Andy's chin quivered, and for a horrifying moment, Gabe thought the kid was going to cry, but he just scratched his nose. "She doesn't believe in Santa. She says no one older'n eight…"

"…believes in Santa Claus." Gabe completed the sentence with resignation. "So what exactly is it you want me to do?"

"Find him," Abby said. "Find the real Santa."

"Then what?" Gabe leaned back in his chair, liking the familiar squeak it made, feeling sorry that the mother of these two kids couldn't let them enjoy something as harmless as Santa Claus. "Do you want me to give him a list of all the toys you want for Christmas?"

Abby looked at her brother, whose serious expression convinced Gabe it wasn't going to be easy to wiggle out of this bargain. "We want you to find Santa for our mom," Andy said. "Because when she sees he's a real person, she'll have to believe in him, and it won't be too late, anymore, and she'll be really happy."

Unselfishness in anyone made Gabe suspicious…and kids were no exception. "So, other than making your mom happy, what else do you two want from old Santa? A pony? A trip to Disney World?"

In one glance, the twins shared a private conversation, and then Abby scooted off the chair. Taking a folded piece of paper from her pocket, she walked around the desk, right up next to Gabe, and held it out for him to see. "I couldn't spell all the words, so I had to draw a picture."

Andy left his chair to come around on Gabe's other side. He pointed to the stick figures on the page. "That's me," he said. "And that's Abby. And that one's Mom."

Abby took over the narration. "And that's our cat, Matilda, and our dog, Sparky. That's Santa Claus and there's his reindeer and that's a real ice-skating rink in the woods, and these are trees beside the house, and here's where we bake cookies, and that's our Christmas tree that we decorated ourselves."

"And that's a turkey, 'cause we don't want to eat spaghetti on Christmas." Andy leaned on the arm of Gabe's chair, feet swinging, face turned upward, his gap-toothed smile eager and excited. "And that's what we want. A *real* Christmas."

"Like the pictures in the magazine." Abby hooked her body over the other chair arm and swung her feet from side to side. "We want a whole week of Christmas."

"May I?" Gabe took the picture from Abby and frowned at the unnamed—and very blue—stick figure. "Who's this?"

Abby checked the drawing. "That's our dad. Except he's not real, 'cause we don't have a dad."

Gabe wondered what had happened to their father and immediately decided that Kate Harmon, whoever she was, was responsible for his absence. After all, any woman who told her children they didn't need a father would be hell to live with. He studied the picture, and then, against his better judgment, he looked in turn at each of the sincere, freckled faces on either side of him. In their eyes, he saw a skepticism far beyond their years…and a hope far beyond their ability to articulate.

He knew he had no business getting mixed up with these two, that he couldn't deliver the *real* Santa, much less their high expectations for a *real* Christmas…whatever that was. But he couldn't recall the last time he'd been asked to do anything so appealing, and he certainly didn't remember the last time he'd considered doing something just to make the world a better place for someone else. Two someones, in this case. Three, if he counted himself. The twins were looking at him as if he were a hero…and he liked it. He liked it a lot. Reaching past the swinging duo, he punched the intercom button on his phone and buzzed Louisa.

"Bring in the contract for detective services," he told her when she answered.

"We don't have a contract for—"

"Ms. Feigle," he said, short-circuiting her denial, "it's all right. You can bring in the *secret* contract."

"The secret contract," she repeated, as if he'd lost his mind.

"Yes, and the pens that write with invisible ink." He punched off the connection and smiled at his new clients. "Well, kiddos, it looks like you've just hired yourselves a real Jack Kass."

Chapter Two

Katherine pulled open the etched-glass entry door of Housley Security, took a deep breath, and stepped inside, reminding herself—*again*—that she could handle Gabe Housley. So he'd kissed her once. Well, actually, she'd kissed him once and he'd kissed her back. It had meant nothing at the time. It certainly meant nothing now, nearly a year later. She barely remembered the incident. There was no doubt in her mind that Gabe had forgotten it ten seconds after it happened.

"May I help you?"

The cheerful voice belonged to the receptionist, a young woman who looked fourteen and was, maybe, twenty-two...at the outside. Katherine had expected as much. Men like Gabe Housley always had clerical pools that were long on looks and short on experience. "I'm Katherine Harmon," she told the girl. "Someone called my office a few minutes ago and said my children were here?"

"Oh, that was me. I'm Wendy. Mr. Housley asked me to call so you wouldn't be worried." Her smile revealed a thin wire retainer across her upper teeth, and Katherine revised her estimated age to under twenty. "They're in his office," Wendy continued, "having their *'pointment*, as Abby called it. Abby, that's your daughter's name, right?" She barely paused for Katherine's affirming nod. "Well, Abby and Andy are just the *cutest* things I've *ever* seen. And *so* grown-up. I mean, they walked right in here and said they needed to see the *detective* of the *house*. Isn't that *cute?* Even Aunt Louisa cracked a smile, and *nobody*—except Mr. Gun—can get *her* to smile."

Something no one would say about Wendy, obviously, as her smile was very much in evidence. Katherine tried to be patient, but she just wanted to get her hands on the *cutest* twins and get the heck out of this office. "Where are they?" she asked.

"In Gabe's—I mean, Mr. Housley's office—finishing their *'pointment*. I'll take you back. The phones aren't that busy, anyway." The phone board beeped several times in annoying succession as Wendy pulled off her headset and pushed back her chair. Still smiling, she motioned for Katherine to follow her down one of the two hallways that angled away from the reception desk, and kept on talking. "It must just be so much *fun* to be the mother of *twins*. They are just *soooo*—"

"Cute." Katherine supplied the adjective this time, and managed to hold the corners of her mouth at a noncommittal slant. "My life would be a waste-land without them."

Wendy nodded her complete understanding. "I can imagine. I'd *love* to have twins. That would be so *cool.* Not now. I mean, I have to get *married* first." She laughed confidingly. "It *does* take two, doesn't it? Have you ever met Gabe? Mr. Housley, I mean. I think he is just *to die for.* And he knows tons of famous people." Her hand floated past a wall of memorabilia, tapping an autographed photo here, a framed newspaper clipping there. "I got to meet Mel Gibson last time he was in New York. He has the most wonderful eyes, you know. Well, here you are...." She stopped talking abruptly and opened a door at the end of the hall.

It wasn't the way Katherine had hoped to make her entrance. In truth, she'd hoped she wouldn't even have to set eyes on the owner of Housley Security. More to the point, she'd hoped he wouldn't get to set eyes on her. But here she was, standing awkwardly in the doorway, staring at him and waiting for the moment when he would look up from where he perched on the corner of his desk and see her.

Not that he would recognize her.

Not that she wanted him to.

But then he turned his head, and there was no mistaking the lightning-quick glint of recognition in his eyes...or the tug of reluctant pleasure at the corners of his mouth. Damn and double damn it, she thought as the stiffening seeped from her knees. She knew it was simply unfortunate that the twins had invaded this office instead of the insurance company on the floor above, but she couldn't understand why she had the consistently bad luck to be attacked by her sexuality every time she saw the man.

Not that her body had ever behaved with the

slightest discernment, but Gabe Housley wasn't even close to being the type of man she usually lusted after. He wasn't some movie star she could weave totally harmless fantasies around. He wasn't even good-looking…although there was something warmly appealing about his eyes. And when his lips quirked in that funny way that wasn't quite a smile, but wasn't exactly a frown, either… Well, she could understand how some women would find that attractive. But not her. And certainly not now.

"So, you're Kate," Gabe said softly, as if there were only the two of them in the room…as if Wendy weren't grinning like Tinker Bell with a new wand as she backed into the hallway and closed the door behind her…as if the silver-haired woman with the sheaf of papers in her hands weren't staring at Katherine with proprietary sternness…as if the twins weren't chattering like Pete and Repeat…as if he, Gabe, had been looking for her, Katherine, all of his life.

Snapping her knees into lock-support position, she lifted her chin and nipped that particular fantasy in the bud. "You have me confused with someone else," she said in a cooler-than-a-peppermint tone of voice. "I'm Katherine Harmon. I'm here to pick up my children."

Her voice brought Abby's head popping into view around the side of one of the chairs, while Andy scrambled to stand on the seat and peer over the hobnailed back of the other.

"Mom!" Abby's eyes widened in alarm.

"Mom!" Andy's astonishment was quickly tempered with a virtuous-sounding "Were you lookin' for us, Mom?"

In the blink of an eye, Abby transformed her expression of surprise into one of angelic innocence. "Bet you're wonderin' what me and Andy are doin' here, aren't ya, Mom?"

"Don't tell, Abby." Andy growled the warning from his superior height. "It's a secret."

"I *know* it's a secret, dummy." She wiggled until her body was hooked like a hairpin around the side of the chair, and the moment she had a clear view of her brother, she stuck out her tongue. "I wasn't going to tell her." She tried to wiggle back around, and would have tipped over if Gabe hadn't reached out to steady the chair.

"Hold on there, Rapunzel," he said. "You're about to fall from your tower."

Abby giggled, and Andy, seeing that his sister was the center of attention, clambered onto the arms of his chair. "Hey, look at me!" he yelled, and prepared to dive over the top.

Moving quickly, Katherine caught him around the waist and set him, feet first, on the floor. "This is an office, not a playground," she said firmly as she grabbed the straps of Abby's pink overalls, lifted her from the chair arm and set her to rights, as well. Then she steeled herself and made actual eye contact with Gabe…just to prove she had no memory whatsoever of kissing him under the mistletoe in this very office last Christmas Eve. "I'm very sorry they bothered you, Mr. Housley. Believe me, it won't happen again."

"It won't? Are you sure?"

Why, she wondered, did she have to notice that his voice was testosterone rich and seductively male? And thick with a humor that, somehow, felt as if it were at her expense? "Of course I'm sure," she answered testily as she herded her progeny toward the door. "I can control my children."

"If this afternoon is any example, I'd say you're being very naive and extremely optimistic."

Katherine turned so fast she nearly toppled the twins...but she didn't let go of Abby's overalls or take her hand off Andy's head. "I beg your pardon?"

Gabe straightened away from the desk, forcing her to remember a few things she'd tried to forget...how tall he was, for one thing, and how broad his shoulders, for another. "I said, if this afternoon is any example, you're being—"

"I heard the rest, Mr. Housley, and I assure you I'm quite capable of keeping my children out of your office." She had to grapple for balance as Abby hopped forward and Andy tried to scrunch out from under her oppressive hand on the other side. "Today just involved an unusual set of circumstances," she continued, as if she were having no problem at all keeping her children under control. "All youngsters get a little overexcited this close to Christmas, but I promise you there's no danger of your seeing Andy and Abby in your office again after today."

Abby halted midhop. Andy stopped squirming. "Yes, he will, too, Mom," Abby informed her for a fact. "He'll see us tomorrow. Me and Andy already got a 'pointment, don't we, Aunt Louisa?"

Katherine's gaze flew to the silver-haired woman, whose smile lit her face in agreement. "Yes, darling, you do," Louisa said.

"No, Abby, you don't." Katherine overruled. "That woman is not your aunt, and you do not have an appointment to see Mr. Housley tomorrow or any other day."

Andy tugged on the seam of her wool slacks. "You can call him Gabe, Mom. He said it was okay. And if you ask real nice, I bet Aunt Louisa would be your aunt, too."

"Maybe..." Abby obviously wasn't keen on that idea. "But Gabe can't be your detective, 'cause we hired him first. And that means we can have a 'pointment anytime we want to. He said so."

"Abby!" Andy exclaimed. "You weren't 'sposed to tell that we hired a detective!"

"I know," she said with a long-suffering roll of her eyes. "But I did it anyway."

Katherine cut her gaze from her daughter's stubborn expression to Andy's earnest face to Gabe's not-so-serious nonsmile. "You hired Mr. Housley to be your detective?" she asked, keeping a suspicious eye on the detective in question.

Andy nodded gravely. "We had to, Mom. We needed a *real* Jack Kass."

Katherine blinked. "You need a donkey?"

"No, Mom." Andy corrected her with an excessively patient sigh. "Not a donkey. A detective. You know, a *Jack Kass.*"

The somber descent of Gabe's brow couldn't begin to disguise his immense enjoyment of the misunderstanding. "Yes," he said in a deeply serious tone. "Apparently, *I* came highly recommended."

That, she could believe. Katherine gave up on restraining the twins, and knelt to their level. "I don't know where you heard the term *jackass,* but—"

"You said it, Mom." Abby was happy to provide the information. "Andy heard you tell somebody that you pay the Jack Kass to find people. Isn't that what detectives do?"

"Yes, but..." She searched for the right way to say this, conscious that Gabe had stooped down to listen in on her explanation. "A detective is a... person, and a jackass is a...donkey."

"A hee-haw donkey?" Abby asked, obviously confused.

Andy's reddish-blond eyebrows scrunched together with a sincere effort to understand. "But... how come you said Gabe was a donkey?"

Two pair of bright blue eyes stared into hers. A pair of brown eyes looked on with considerable interest. Katherine cleared her throat and managed a patently false chuckle. "You misunderstood, sweetheart. I'm sure that isn't what I said."

"Yes, it is," Andy assured her. "It is what you said. I heard you."

"He did, Mom." Abby, for once, sided with her brother. "And you always tell the truth, so Gabe must be a donkey and a Jack Kass, just like you said."

Katherine met Gabe's look of inquisitive amuse-

ment with a sinking heart, then turned to the only
other person in the room who might know what it
was like to be a mother, and therefore lend her support. "Children," she said to Louisa, in a pitifully
embarrassing attempt to shift some of the blame.
"They sometimes get words all mixed up, don't
they? Who knows where they hear these things."

"Little pitchers have big ears" was Louisa's dry
and unsympathetic comment. She rapped the papers
against the desktop and patted them into precise order as she marched to the door. "And big pitchers
have big mouths," she said in leaving.

"Hmm..." Gabe said. "An astute observation."

"She doesn't mean you have a big mouth, Mom,"
Andy explained, as seriously as if he were interpret-
ing at the United Nations. "And she doesn't mean
me and Abby have big ears. She means you're a
good talker and me and Abby are good list'ners and
that's how come we found out all about detectives
bein' donkeys and Jack Kasses." He gave her a
heartwarming gap-toothed grin. "We learned it all
from you, Mom."

Gabe remained stooped, his knees not an inch
from hers, his expression seriously amused, his body
as solidly balanced as hers was unsteady, his eyes
sparkling with laughter. "I commend you, Kate, for
instructing your children in the finer distinctions of
the English language."

"My name is Katherine," she corrected coolly.
"A distinction surely even a...*detective* can understand." Her legs were trembling with protest at her
crouched position, but she'd rather hobble around at

waist height for the rest of her life than let him think his nearness unnerved her.

"You know, *Katherine*," he said, the corner of his mouth lifting in pensive delight, "I have this feeling you don't like me much, but I can't figure out why. Were we lovers in a past life, maybe?"

Lovers! Ha! She straightened as if she had springs attached to her feet. "That, certainly, would explain why I might dislike you, but as it happens, Mr. Housley, until ten minutes ago, when I walked in here, I didn't know you well enough to either like or dislike you."

"And now?" He straightened slowly, holding her gaze as he did so...which irritated her for a bunch of reasons, none of them coherent. "Have you come to a conclusion?"

"Oh, yes."

He stepped nearer, coming a little too close for her comfort. "And that is...?"

Her legs tingled after being cramped so long, but she'd stand still if it killed her. "My conclusion, Mr. Housley..."

"Please, call me Gabe," he said, interrupting her. "Andy said it was okay."

"Andy doesn't get a vote, *Mr. Housley*. As I was saying..." A sudden lack of background noise alerted her and Katherine glanced down at the twins, noting their uncharacteristic stillness and realizing that she was the focus of their concentrated attention. The little monkeys were probably absorbing every nuance of her body language and tone of voice so that they could repeat what she said and how she said it at a later—and inopportune—moment. "My conclusion is that I should take my children upstairs to my office and you should mind your own business."

"Ah, Kate, that presents a problem. You became my business, you see, when I agreed to take the twins' case."

"What case?" Annoyance snapped and crackled in her voice. "They're seven years old. They don't need a detective. And even if they did, they can't just walk into a security company and *hire* one!"

"But we did, Mom." Andy patted her arm comfortingly. "We hired Gabe to find Santa Claus."

Santa Claus! The fat old scoundrel was haunting her today. Katherine grabbed Andy's hand and cast Gabe a black glance. "Well, Mr. Housley can't find Santa Claus, because Santa Claus doesn't exist. And I don't want to hear another word about it."

"But, Mom!" Abby took a position closer to Gabe than her mother. "We gave him all our cash! Five whole dollars!"

Katherine's gaze swung ruthlessly to Gabe. "You took their money?"

He shrugged, without even the grace to look ashamed. "They didn't bring their checkbook."

Pursing her lips, Katherine decided nothing but mischief could come of letting this Santa business continue any further. She was going to end it before Gabe gave the twins further encouragement and completely undermined her authority. "Taking lunch money from children makes you a bully, Mr. Housley, not a businessman."

Gabe frowned at Andy. "Was that your *lunch* money?"

"Nope." Andy shook his head. "Abby and me got 'spelled, so we don't need no lunch money."

"Spelled?" Gabe repeated.

"Any money," Katherine corrected automatically. "You don't need any lunch money."

"That's what I said." Andy tugged his hand free. "You know, Gabe, *'spelled.*"

"We're dink-quints," Abby explained with a dramatic gesture. "We got kicked out of Saint Julian's."

"You're not delinquents." Katherine began, although no one appeared to be listening to her. "And you didn't get kicked out of school. You were given extra vacation days, that's all."

"Yep," Andy said. "We got kicked out of school 'cause we didn't believe in Santa Claus."

Katherine decided it was time to assume control of the conversation and her children. "Look, it doesn't matter what the money was intended for," she explained to the twins. "Mr. Housley took it under false pretenses, and he needs to return it."

Gabe crossed his arms at his chest. "I'm afraid I can't. We've already signed the contract."

Abby nodded happily. "A secret contract."

"With invisible ink." Andy added.

"How convenient." Katherine glared at Gabe, noting, despite her best intentions, that he had warm, wonderful eyes. The color of aged Scotch and rich with laughter.

Except this was no laughing matter.

Gathering a twin's hand in each of her own, she held her ground and her temper. "I think you'd better explain to Abby and Andy that you were only teasing," she said stiffly. "Tell them you're not a detective, this isn't a detective agency, and that they did not hire you."

"I wish I could, Kate."

The nickname sounded appallingly intimate, and Katherine raised her brows in rebuttal.

"I tried to talk them out of this idea," he continued. "But they're very determined youngsters, as I'm sure you're aware. And, frankly, now that I've had a little time to observe you, I believe they're right."

Katherine didn't want to ask, but the words were out of her mouth before she could stop them. "Right about what?"

He looked at her with sympathy in his eyes. "That you missed your chance and now you're too old to believe in Santa Claus."

"Old? *I'm* too old?" She pulled her shoulders back in a barely conscious defensive gesture. "That's ridiculous."

He nodded. "That's exactly what I said."

Realizing where this was headed, she made a belated correction. "I meant it's ridiculous to be having this discussion. There is no such person as Santa Claus, and my age has nothing to do with it."

"You're sure about that?"

"Of course I'm sure," she snapped.

"The twins and I disagree."

"You may, but they don't." She looked down at the upturned faces of her son and daughter. "Haven't

I always told you the truth?'' she asked. ''Haven't I always been perfectly honest with you?''

''Well, sure, Mom,'' Andy acknowledged. ''But Gabe believes in Santa. We asked him.''

''And I'm sure he told you that Santa Claus is real.'' She sighed. ''I've explained this to you and Abby a dozen times. Adults sometimes say things because they think children can't understand the truth. Mr. Housley was merely saying what he believed you wanted to hear.''

''I did want to hear it, Mom. I really did.''

''Andy. Just because we want something to be true doesn't mean it is. You know that, don't you?''

Andy's chin dropped onto his chest. Abby sniffled. And Katherine felt worse than awful…as if *she* were the one filling their heads with nonsense. Her chin rose with her anger, and she leveled both at the man before her. ''Do you see what you've done?'' she said irritably. ''We're leaving now, but in the future, I suggest you be more careful what you say to innocent children, or you may find yourself defending your 'beliefs' in a court of law.''

Gabe stroked the pad of his thumb along his jawline and regarded her, still with amusement. ''That sounded a little like a threat.''

''An astute observation.'' Turning, she moved the twins ahead of her and marched them toward the door.

''Are you implying you'd sue me because I told your children that I believe in Santa Claus?''

It sounded silly, put like that. But then, everything

about Santa Claus was silly. "I wasn't implying anything. I was stating a fact."

"You're not serious."

"Keep your ideas and ideals away from my children, Mr. Housley, or you'll discover just how serious I am."

He followed the three of them into the front office. The phone beeped with unanswered calls, but Wendy's attention was firmly fixed on the procession that was heading for the door. Moving ahead, Gabe paused with his hand on the doorknob. "Let me be sure I understand you. Are you saying, you'll hire a lawyer and file a legal action to stop me from saying I believe in Santa?"

"No," she said calmly, although her heart was pounding with irritation. "I'd hire a lawyer and file a legal action to keep you from polluting the minds of my children with lies."

He lowered his brows in a thoughtful frown. "You wouldn't. File something as ridiculous as a *Santa suit?*" He shook his head, obviously having convinced himself. "You'd be laughed out of the courthouse. I can see you now, trying to explain to the judge exactly which one of us is Mr. Scrooge."

She raised her brows to contradict the lowering of his. "That would be *Miss* Scrooge to you. Now, if you'll be so helpful as to open the door, my children and I will be out of your way."

He obliged with a flourish, and Katherine guided the twins through the doorway with the sure knowledge that she was making a narrow escape and the unsettling realization that he knew it, too.

"Bye, Gabe." Oblivious to the tension, Andy waved cheerfully with the hand Katherine didn't have clamped in her own.

"Bye, Gabe." Abby waved, too. "See ya tomorrow."

Katherine guided them inside the cantankerous old elevator, which, for once, opened at the first touch of the call button. Pride turned her face front and kept her chin up as she met Gabe's eyes across the width of the hallway. The slant of his lips unnerved her, and she felt she had to say something. "I expect you to return the money."

"Do you, Kate?" His voice evoked a sudden, troublesome memory of the kiss he didn't remember and she hadn't been able to forget. "I expect you'll have to wait and see what tomorrow brings."

"Tomorrow will bring colder temperatures and a chance of snow," she said with a pleasantly confident smile. "Other than that, there'll be no surprises."

"You underestimate me, Kate," he called as the elevator doors creaked and began to close.

She lifted her shoulder in an indifferent shrug. "Goodbye, Mr. Housley. Have yourself a very merry Christmas."

It was a fitting last word, she thought, feeling rather pleased with how she'd handled the situation and the man. But then, just as the doors rattled shut, Gabe began to sing, his lusty baritone sneaking inside the elevator like a pesky gnat.

Katherine didn't think fast enough to plug her ears before the twins picked up the tune, and their enthusiastic voices serenaded her all the way up with a particularly exuberant rendition of "Santa Claus Is Coming to Town!"

Chapter Three

The Knicks were playing basketball the way the game was meant to be played, maintaining their seven-point lead, basket by basket. Consequently the home fans showed their appreciation in a raucous, stomp-the-feet excitement that occasionally generated a wave of support. When the latest semichoreographed cheer rippled across the grandstand, Gabe followed his father to his feet in fluid homage, then sat again as the wave passed on.

"Hell of a game, Junior!" Gun slapped Gabe on the knee and leaned forward to eagle-eye the fourth-quarter tip-off. "Remind me to buy a ticket next time."

"Why would you do that?" Gabe said dryly, as he watched the Knicks take control of the ball. "You always use my extra one, anyway."

"True, but if I got one of my own, I could bring a friend."

"Great idea, Dad. Exactly what I had in mind when I bought these two tickets. As a matter of fact, I had a friend all picked out to bring with me this evening."

"Friend. Humph." Gun dismissed the plans he'd forced Gabe to change by showing up at the office in time to wangle a ticket...and a tuna sandwich...out of his only child. "That Marsha person may have bamboozled you into believing she's crazy about basketball, but she doesn't fool me for a minute. She wouldn't know the difference between a rim shot and a ringtoss. And she's too tall for you, Junior."

"Her name is Michelle, Dad. And she's five-eleven. I'm taller by a good three inches."

"Well, I'm not, and I'll be damned if you're going to marry some amazon I'd have to spend the rest of my life looking up to."

"I don't want to marry her. I just want to take her to a basketball game."

"You're well out of it, Junior. I'm telling you, Marsha doesn't like basketball, no matter what she says." Gun cupped his hands around his mouth and yelled, "Hey, ref! If you had another eye, you'd be a Cyclops!" He threw his hands up in anguished sportsmanship. "Did you *see* that?" he asked the crowd in general. "If that player's elbow had been a wrecking ball, there'd be bodies all over the court! Come on, ref! Get a magnifying glass!"

There was a brief altercation between the referee and the Knicks' coach, which Gun encouraged with several pithy remarks, but when no one got kicked out of the game, he settled back with a sigh. "Louisa tells me you've agreed to do a little detective work for a couple of grade-school dropouts."

It was amazing, Gabe thought. Louisa didn't look

like the gossipy sort. Lord knew, she never told *him* anything. But Gun could be out of the office for days on end and still know everything that had gone on in his absence. It was part of his persona as *The Detective.* "Yes," Gabe said. "I have Louisa to thank for that little practical joke. She says she didn't, but I know she set up the whole thing. Locked me in my office with a couple of redheaded brats, and the next thing I knew, I was putting my John Henry on a secret contract with invisible ink."

Gun managed to look away from the action long enough to bestow a quizzical frown on him. "I thought you didn't like kids."

"It's not that I don't like them, I just don't know that I want one calling me Daddy, that's all."

"Good thing for you I didn't feel that way, huh?"

"It's harder raising children in this day and age," Gabe said sagely. "There's a lot more responsibility."

"Oh, yes, I forgot. Everything's more difficult for *your* generation." Gun's bushy salt-and-pepper eyebrows angled into sarcastic upside-down vees. "Snap out of it, Junior. Many more sorry excuses like that and I'll be forced to adopt a couple of grandkids to fill my lonely hours."

"Lonely hours, my a—"

"Don't be vulgar. You don't want people to think you're a jackass."

Gabe frowned. "Louisa told you that, too, I suppose."

"Don't recall where I heard it."

"Mmm-hmm..." Gabe had heard that before...many times. If nothing else, Gun had a very convenient memory. "Why don't you just tell me anything she left out, and I'll fill in the blanks for you."

A whistle blew, and with a whoop of outrage, Gun surged to his feet, pumping the air with his fist. "Whattayamean, *foul?*" he yelled. "If that was a foul, I'm Mother Teresa!" He turned to commiserate with a red-faced fan on his other side. "Where do they get these referees? The dark side of the moon?"

Gabe crossed his arms and tried to get back into the spirit of the game. After all, he'd shelled out quite a few bucks for these tickets. But all he could think about was the five crumpled dollar bills in his shirt pocket, and Katherine Harmon. Both images created a warm spot near his heart. For reasons known only to God...and possibly Gun.

"So you're going to help a couple of industrious kids find Santa Claus." Gun resumed his seat on the bleachers and picked up the conversation again. "A commendable bit of charity, Junior. I'm proud of you for taking the case."

"I'm not. Taking the case, that is. I'm returning their money tomorrow."

"What for? Don't tell me you're scared of two seven-year-old kids."

"No, I'm not scared of two seven-year-old kids," Gabe parroted in denial. "Their mother is scary enough for me, thanks. She threatened to sue me."

Gun looked momentarily concerned. "Not a former client of mine, is she?"

"You're in the clear on this one. She doesn't believe in Santa Claus, and doesn't think anyone else should, either.''

"So she's going to sue you? What for? Does she think you own stock in Christmas?''

"I know. She was being ridiculous, and I told her so, too.''

"Oh, I'm sure that calmed her right down.'' Gun stroked his clipped white beard and shook his head. "She was probably tickled pink you pointed that out to her.''

"All right, so it might not have been the most tactful way to tell her she was overreacting. But from the moment she walked in the room, I had this feeling she didn't think much of me, even before she found out I'd agreed to help the twins look for Santa.'' Gabe bent forward, clasping his hands between his knees. "I'm almost certain we've never officially met, but she seemed very familiar, somehow. And it wasn't the kind of familiar feeling you get from passing someone in the lobby a few times, either. It was more like...well, almost as if I knew things about her I had no way of knowing. And I know what you're thinking, but she's not the kind of woman I'd forget.''

"Have you asked Louisa?''

Gabe let his mouth quirk in a wry smile. "Believe it or not, Dad, there are a few things even Louisa doesn't know.''

"If there's a woman out there who wants to sue you and Louisa doesn't know about it, you'd better get yourself a lawyer.''

"Katherine doesn't want to sue me. That was just her way of...well, of warning me off."

"Doesn't want you around her kids, huh?"

"The funny thing is, I think the warning was more personal than that. I think she's afraid of me." Gabe wasn't sure where that insight had come from, but he knew as soon as he said it that he was right. It was the angle he'd been trying to find all evening, the reason Katherine had been so ill at ease in his office. Despite the circumstances—even cutting her some slack for the anxiety she must have felt when she discovered that her children had wandered away from her office and wound up in his—she'd been abnormally nervous.

He hadn't imagined it. He knew he hadn't. But he couldn't think of a thing to account for it, either. Katherine Harmon didn't like him. And it wasn't just a general dislike of men. It was real and it was personal. She didn't like *him*. Until this minute, though, it hadn't occurred to him that he scared her. Scared her in the same way kids had always scared him. Not because he found them frightening creatures, but because he found them fascinating, and some survivalist instinct told him he had to steer clear or get involved.

So Katherine Harmon was afraid of him. Interesting. A woman who didn't believe in Santa Claus, who said she believed a father was unnecessary—or at least nonessential—in a child's life, a woman who probably didn't allow many men into her and her children's lives, was afraid of getting involved with him. She didn't want anyone to hurt Abby and Andy, which was perfectly understandable. Except they got hurt either way, didn't they?

In his mind, he could see their wistful blue eyes, and he knew he was their last hope. Well, okay, maybe the situation wasn't that desperate, but there wouldn't be many more opportunities for them to have a Christmas like the one in their drawing. In another year, they'd be older, and there'd be fewer people who'd bother to pretend that Santa was real. And over time, they'd develop that cynical outer shell of protection, that Santa-is-for-kids, hurry-up-and-just-get-through-the-holidays mentality of adults, and Christmas would lose much, if not all, of its magic. As it already had for their mother.

Gabe looked at his father, at the hair that was now sparse and white, at the accumulated wrinkles, and at the faded brown eyes that had yet to lose their mischievous sparkle. "Do you still believe in Santa Claus, Dad?"

"Hell, yes. And I've asked for a Snow Flyer sled this year, so when you see it under the tree, don't go thinking it's yours."

Gabe laughed. "I'll trade you a day with your Snow Flyer for a ticket to the next Knicks game."

"What kind of deal is that? You'd give me the ticket anyway."

For a moment, the action on the court held their combined attention. "Dad?" Gabe asked. "If you had to go looking for Santa Claus, where would you start?"

"Macy's," Gun said decisively. "And from there, I'd just follow my instincts."

"What if your instincts were telling you to run like hell?"

"Then I'd know I was on the right track." Gun offered an encouraging nudge with his elbow. "Just out of curiosity, though, how are you planning to persuade a woman who, in your words, 'doesn't think much of you,' to let you hang around long enough to prove there really is a Santa Claus?"

"I haven't the faintest idea."

Gun's short white beard dipped toward his chest in a satisfied nod. "Now you're beginning to talk like a real detective."

KATHERINE STIRRED a teaspoonful of gourmet flavoring into her coffee and inhaled the aroma as she carried the cup and saucer with her into the living room. Tucking her legs under her, she sank onto the sofa and into the luxury of a morning at home. Not that she didn't have work to do; she'd brought a pile of it with her from the office yesterday. But while the twins were still asleep and the day was still fairly new, she could relax and enjoy a few minutes of peace and quiet. And a leisurely cup of coffee, one of the small pleasures of life she allowed herself. The only one she absolutely refused to feel guilty about.

Closing her eyes, she brought her favorite china cup to her lips, anticipating the first hot, slightly bitter taste of the coffee. The door buzzer scalded her solitude in a noisy interruption, and a splash of coffee slopped onto the collar of her white terry robe. Dabbing at it with one end of the robe's tie belt, she carried the cup with her to the front door of the apartment. She flipped back the cover of the peephole, looked out, and stepped back so fast she subsequently spilled coffee dowr the other lapel and onto the cotton nightgown underneath. What the hell was *he* doing here?

The buzzer blared again and, angrily, she threw back the locks and jerked open the door. "Mr. Housley," she said. "What do you want?"

He smiled, and her stupid heart stuttered like a lovesick adolescent. "Coffee," he said easily, as if he showed up at her door every morning to join her in a cup. "I feel naked until I've spilled some on my shirt." His gaze shifted from her stained lapels to the cup in her hand. "Can you spare a few drops?"

"How did you get up here?"

He hooked his thumb toward the hallway behind him. "I got into the elevator and punched in your floor. From there, I just had to walk down the hall until I reached your apartment."

How anyone so obnoxious could look so attractive at this hour, Katherine couldn't understand. The few times she'd been with a man at this time of day had not been conducive to noticing such things as the way his hair waved away from his forehead...except for that one stray lock that fell forward. She certainly had no reason or desire to notice his clean, obviously freshly shaven face, or that his eyes were the same shade of whiskey brown as his Armani overcoat. The coat fell casually from his shoulders, angling toward the back on the right side, as if it were accustomed to being pushed aside in order for him to reach the pocket of his tweed slacks. This morning, he looked the way he had the first time she saw him. Only he hadn't been standing still then. He'd been striding through the lobby of the Fitzpatrick Building as if he owned the place. She'd subsequently discovered that he did...own the place, that is. She'd also, subsequently, decided that it wasn't the man she found attractive at all. It was his coat...the one he was wearing now. "How did you get past the security guard downstairs?"

"Raymond?" Gabe said the name easily and with great familiarity. "Oh, I've known him for ages. He works for me."

"You being Housley Security, I suppose."

He nodded, adopting an expression she felt sure was meant to appear humble. "It isn't quite as personal as it sounds," he said. "We provide the security personnel and monitor the alarm systems for a lot of apartment buildings. I just happen to know Raymond because he's played in a monthly poker game with my dad for...well, for a lot of years."

It figured. Katherine wished abruptly that she'd bought an apartment on the Upper East Side instead of this Central Park location. Although Housley Security had probably infiltrated there, as well. "Do you hire all of your father's poker buddies to fill security positions?"

"Only the winners. The losers have to work in the main office."

"How reassuring," she said, feeling unreasonably annoyed by the knowledge that whether she was at her office or at home in her apartment, her security was connected to Gabe Housley.

"I lost one game too many and ended up as president of the company," he said modestly.

She offered a pseudosmile in reply and managed to throttle the impulse to rub at the stains on her lapels. "I'm surprised you're still in business, if you don't insist your security personnel notify tenants *before* allowing a visitor upstairs."

"Oh, that's standard procedure, as I'm sure you know." He tightened his lips and, either by intent or design, came up with that quirk of a smile she found so irritating...and so irrationally appealing. "But this morning I pulled rank and told Raymond he didn't need to buzz me through. I figured the twins might be still asleep and the noise might wake them."

She leaned her shoulder against the door, wondering what he wanted and why she didn't just insist he spit it out. "When I file my complaint with the residents' association, I'll be sure to mention you broke the rules out of a sincere consideration for my kids and their need for sleep." She knew she wasn't going to file a complaint, and he undoubtedly knew it, too. But she felt she had to at least raise the point. "Maybe poor Raymond won't lose his job."

"Raymond isn't in any danger of losing his job."

"Well, I can't imagine that *your* head would be the one to roll."

He impatiently brushed the hair back from his forehead. "You know, Kate, I didn't come here to argue."

"We're not arguing, Mr. Housley...although we will be if you keep calling me Kate."

"Katherine, then."

She liked the way he said her name, but then, she liked the frustration she saw gathering in his eyes, too. "Now that I think about it," she continued. "There's really no reason for you to call me anything at all. Have a nice day, and the next time you decide to pay an unexpected visit, I suggest you have the guard follow the standard procedure and announce your impending arrival."

"I didn't think you'd invite me to come up if I did."

"You're absolutely right. I wouldn't have." She started to close the door, but Gabe flattened a hand against the panel to keep it open. "I'd really like to talk to you, if you think you can get that chip off your shoulder long enough to hear me out."

Chip? He thought *she* had a chip on *her* shoulder? "You mean you're not going to 'pull rank' and just knock it off yourself?"

"I'm actually a very gentle man most of the time. It's only when I can't figure out why someone dislikes me as intensely as you apparently do that I get a bit testy."

"Happens often, does it?"

"No," he said, his voice getting testier by the syllable. "It happens so infrequently that it really bugs me. So why don't you just tell me what it is about me that puts you up on such a high horse, and I'll apologize for whatever it is I did or didn't do. Then, perhaps, you can offer me a cup of coffee, and we can sit down and talk civilly."

Katherine wished, irrelevantly, that she'd put on makeup and combed her hair. Not that it made a bit of difference. Regardless of how she looked, she was going to invite him in and offer him a cup of coffee, because it was obvious he wasn't going away until she did. "Would you like to come inside and have a cup of coffee?" she asked, using the element of surprise to her advantage. "I think you and I need to come to an understanding."

He frowned at her sudden change of tactic, but stepped inside quickly, as if he thought she might change her mind. "Thank you," he said.

She closed the door and enjoyed a moment of serene confidence—until she turned around and looked straight at his broad chest, covered with a blue coarsely woven shirt, striped with a Jerry Garcia necktie and outlined by the lapels of that damn overcoat. In the same way a mist of rain saturates the atmosphere on a hot summer day, a sensual attraction soaked into her awareness, and the air around her went from morning fresh to humid in a single breath. She was an idiot to have invited him into her home, an idiot to think she could sit and talk to him as if he were the guy next door. But she could hardly retract her invitation now without revealing what an idiot she was. So she'd just hear what he had to say and get him out of the apartment before she started noticing other intriguing things about him, beyond his overcoat.

"You can put your coat over there." She gestured blindly, not caring where he put it, as long as he took it off. "Can I get you some coffee?" Without waiting for his answer, she headed for the kitchen and wondered if it would lower her body temperature any if she slipped a couple of ice cubes down the neck of her robe. But he followed her, and even if she wanted to, she couldn't have iced herself without him noticing. "Sugar? Cream?" she asked. "I have some International Flavors, too, if you like."

"Black," he said. "I figure if I'm going to drink the stuff, I shouldn't cover up the taste with artificial sweeteners and gourmet flavorings."

Just like that, guilt attached itself to her sugared, creamed and gourmet-flavored indulgence, and she wanted to put her hands over her own cup, so that he couldn't see the betraying caramel color. Instead, she took a mug from the cabinet and filled it with coffee, noting with some small satisfaction that she'd randomly chosen a cup inscribed with the words *Men! Who needs them?* She handed it to him, noting that he looked marginally less attractive out of the coat than in it, but she was still careful to avoid any hand-to-hand contact as he took the mug.

To her dismay, instead of returning to the other room, he leaned a shoulder against the door frame and proceeded to sip the coffee, his brown eyes leisurely taking in the dirty dishes in the sink, the smear of grape jelly on the counter, the smudgy fingerprints on the refrigerator...and her, all sixty-four-and-a-half inches of her at her disheveled, stained, only-recently-rolled-out-of-bed and frumpy best. Imagining the scene through his eyes, Katherine felt about as uncomfortable as she'd ever felt in her own kitchen...not counting the time she burned the oatmeal.

"I like your taste in art." He nodded at the crayon

drawings magnetically tacked to the refrigerator and Scotch-taped on cabinet doors. "I even recognize the artists."

She glanced fondly at the first-grade decor. "It probably helps that they print their names in really big letters."

"I think the subject matter would give them away, even without the signatures." Pointing to one of several neatly drawn pictures, he indicated the objects in turn. "That would be Abby, Andy, and you, a house, Sparky the dog, and..." He paused, obviously trying to recall the name of the cat and looking to her for help.

"Matilda the cat," Katherine supplied. "I see you were with the twins long enough yesterday to learn the entire menagerie."

"Right down to the Slime Monster, the Trash Monster, and the Alien Wearing Underpants."

She glanced at Andy's collection of monsters, all drawn in quick, vivid, one-color strokes of crayon, and shook her head. "I hope he outgrows this monster fixation soon. Every time I walk into the kitchen, it seems like there's a new one that's stranger than the one before it."

"Nothing strange about it. Boys love ugly, gross and scary things. It's the nature of the male, the way we learn to deal with fear."

"Really?" She narrowed her eyes, thinking the true nature of males was basically anything that was directly opposite of the female. "Are you afraid of monsters?"

"Not anymore." He sipped the coffee and regarded her over the rim of the mug. "If I had to draw the things I'm most afraid of, the picture would be closer to Abby's than Andy's. What about you, Kate...Katherine? What are you afraid of?"

"Wasting the only quiet time I'm likely to get today." Leaving her china cup on the counter, she stepped toward him, thinking he'd take the hint and back out of the way.

He didn't. He kept his shoulder pressed against the doorjamb and continued to lean like the Tower of Pisa, holding the mug easily in the curve of his large hand, watching her with more interest than her appearance merited. She arched her brows in a subtle warning. "Are you going to spill that on your shirt yourself, or could I be of some assistance?"

Gabe laughed, and a warm, welcoming response rose in her throat. She choked it back, pointing out to her foolish heart that not only was he arrogant, pushy and irritating, he had undoubtedly kissed a dozen women last Christmas Eve and probably didn't remember half of them. Realizing she was obviously in the forgettable half, she frowned and squared her shoulders. "Let's go in the other room," she said firmly. "Then you can say your piece and leave."

His eyebrows drew together in a startled frown as he glanced from her to the coffee mug in his hand. "Do I get to finish my coffee before you kick me out?"

"If you drink fast, you do." She took a second wary step toward the doorway, acutely aware that he took up too much space in her kitchen and that he didn't seem in a hurry to leave. But when he did

vacate the doorway and walk into the open space of
the combined dining and living areas, she abruptly
missed the intimacy of the smaller room. Which was
annoying.

Skirting the dining room table, she crossed the
room and took a seat on the couch, curling her feet
on the cushion and tucking her robe around her legs
and toes. She looked up suddenly and caught him
watching her...and a ribbon of possibility wound like
Christmas tinsel through her consciousness, pretty
but insubstantial. With a nod, she indicated that he
should sit down. He glanced from the empty place
beside her on the sofa and then to the overstuffed
chair and ottoman, obviously debating where to sit.
As if she couldn't be more unconcerned, Katherine
slipped one foot out from under cover and stretched
one leg across the sofa, making an elaborate gesture
of readjusting the terry robe so that her bare leg was
covered, while effectively taking away the option of
sitting beside her.

With a shrug, Gabe settled into the overstuffed
chair and sank into the shaped softness until his
knees rose nearly level with his chest and his body
formed a lazy *N* in the chair. He looked surprised
and none too comfortable as he met her gaze across
the coffee table. "You might have warned me this
was a man-eating chair. Or is this how you get rid
of all your unwanted guests?"

"Only the larger ones," she said, unable to keep
the laughter out of her voice. "The twins like to sit
there when they watch television, but I have to admit,

I've never seen them disappear quite so far down into it."

"They probably don't sit still long enough to sink." Holding the mug high and steady, he tried to wrestle his way up from the depths, but halfway out, he gave up and slowly submerged again. "Now, aren't you sorry you didn't ask me to sit beside you? I may be stuck in this chair for the rest of my life, which means you'll be stuck with me as a fixture in your living room for the rest of yours."

"That won't be a problem," she said pleasantly. "I'll hire some movers, and they'll get you right out of here."

"Do you always have an immediate solution to your problems, Katherine?"

"I don't deal well with uncertainty," she said. "And I'm not terribly patient, so why don't you tell me why you're here?"

As if he needed to recall the reason, he took another lingering sip of coffee. "I could say I came to return the twins' five dollars..."

"But that wouldn't be the truth," she deduced.

He lifted his shoulder in a wry shrug. "I'm not going to spend it, if that's what worries you, and I'll give it back after this contract thing is resolved...which is one of the reasons I wanted to see you this morning."

From long practice, Katherine picked up the pivotal word. "What contract?"

"The Santa contract," he said with a smile. "That's what we're calling it around the office."

"I suppose that would be the secret contract the three of you signed with invisible ink."

"That would be the one, yes. I thought you and I should discuss the terms."

"You want to discuss a contract that doesn't exist?"

"It exists. I have a copy in my office."

"Let's not quibble over technicalities. The contract isn't real, no matter how many copies you have."

"It's real to Andy and Abby," he pointed out candidly. "They want to find Santa Claus. What's so wrong with that?"

"Wrong?" she repeated, as if his mistake were blatantly obvious. "What's wrong is that there isn't a Santa Claus to find."

"But what if I could prove to you that there is?"

"You'd be a magician, and even then it would still be a trick, because Santa Claus isn't real."

"Not in your experience."

She pursed her lips. "Not in anyone's experience. He's fiction, a fairy tale, nonexistent. Period. End of story."

"But what if I could prove you're wrong?"

"Trust me on this. If you're determined to work miracles, put your energy into creating world peace. With that, at least, you'd have a fighting chance of success."

Humor sparked in his eyes. "What did Santa Claus ever do to you, Katherine?"

"It's what I did to him, Gabe." His name just slipped out, and it hung there between them, an intimacy she hadn't intended, a note of warmth she hoped he hadn't noticed. "I grew up and I outgrew fantastical stories about a fat old elf in a red suit with a long white beard."

"So you did believe in him...once."

"Maybe. I honestly don't remember."

He seemed to see that for the lie it was, because he slumped more comfortably in the chair and looked perfectly satisfied. "Let me guess. One Christmas when you were...oh, not quite eight years old, you asked Santa for something, a doll, maybe, and he didn't deliver and you never forgave him."

"You've been watching Frank Capra movies, haven't you? Or that sappy old *Miracle on 34th Street.*"

"I watch it every year. It wouldn't be Christmas without being able to cheer when the post office delivers all that mail to Kris Kringle, proving he's the real Santa Claus. I'm a faithful fan."

"It figures."

"Yes, it does," he said with that odd quirk of his lips. "I'll even admit I get a tear in my eye at the end, when they discover Kris's cane in the corner of their dream house."

"And, I suppose, you cry at the end of *It's a Wonderful Life,* too."

"Are you kidding? When the bell rings and Jimmy Stewart knows Clarence got his wings..." Gabe sighed dramatically. "That scene has me reaching for another hankie every time." The quirk grew into a sad smile. "I'll bet you don't even cry in *A Christ-*

mas Carol, when Tiny Tim says, 'God bless us every one!'"

Her lips tightened, despite her express desire to look amused at his expense. "I'm not a Scrooge. I just don't get emotionally involved with movies. I rarely even watch them."

"So what was it, Katherine? The gift you asked Santa for but never got?"

She traced a random design on the sofa arm. "A pony."

"A pony? Really? Me too. I've always felt Dad made some kind of deal with Santa that year, insisting I'd really said puppy, instead of pony. But I got the puppy, and when you're seven, a puppy's just as great as a pony, anyway." He shook his head sympathetically. "I guess you didn't get either one, huh?"

"I was being facetious when I said that, Mr. Housley. I assumed you'd know it was a joke."

"You shouldn't joke about Santa Claus, Kate...and don't bother to tell me that isn't your name, because until you stop calling me *Mr. Housley,* I'm calling you whatever I want."

Katherine narrowed her eyes. "Maybe you should call me long-distance, *Gabe?* Or better yet—"

"Mom?" The interruption was followed by the *pat, pat, patter* of bunny house slippers slapping the wood floor as Abby walked over and climbed up on the sofa, nestling into Katherine's side like a sleepy kitten. "Hi, Gabe," she said, then held up a scraggly, loosely stuffed orange lion. "This is Matilda. She doesn't talk."

"Good morning, Abby," he said. "Good morning, Matilda." With a frown, his gaze turned from the bedraggled lion to Katherine. "I thought Matilda was the name of your cat?"

"Lions are cats," Abby explained with a yawn. "And they don't shred."

"Shed," Katherine said, tucking her arm around Abby's warm shoulders. "And real lions probably do shed...and shred, but we like Matilda just the way she is, don't we, sweetie?"

Abby let go and the stuffed animal plopped onto Katherine's lap. "I'd like her better if she was real, Mom, 'cause then I could brush her and dress her in pretty clothes and listen to her purr."

It was an old discussion, and one Katherine had no intention of reopening. "Did you have sweet dreams?"

"Mmm-hmm. When are we going? I can go tell Andy to wake up, if it's time."

Abby looked expectantly at Gabe and Katherine felt a twinge of possessive alarm. Before he could give her daughter some perfectly ridiculous answer, she jumped in with a confident "We're not going anywhere until this afternoon."

Abby looked up in surprise, her eyes widening with suspicion. "You're gonna go with us?"

"Of course. You and Andy can't go to the museum all by yourselves, now, can you?"

"Oh." Abby's stricken gaze flew to Gabe. "I thought we were gonna go look for Santa Claus."

Katherine arched her brows at the half man, half

chair across from her. "Now where would you get an idea like that, Abby?" she asked coolly.

"Gabe said. He said he'd take us to look for the real Santa Claus today, didn't you, Gabe?"

"He was teasing, Abby. You know there's no such thing as a real Santa Claus."

Gabe made an effort to sit straighter. "I wasn't teasing," he said. "I told them they could help me look for Santa."

"See, Mom? He meant it. He said we could help him look, and he meant it. It was a promise."

"Well, he shouldn't have promised any such thing without checking with me." She glared at the "he" under discussion. "You had no right to offer them any kind of outing without getting my permission first. You're virtually a stranger."

"No, he isn't, Mom." Abby stated firmly. "He's a *real* detective and me and Andy hired him, and we can go anywhere we want to with him."

Katherine blinked, startled by the defiance in her daughter's usually very reasonable voice. "Don't talk to me in that tone of voice, Abigail Grace. Remember, I'm the mother and *you're* the child."

Abby sighed as she retrieved Matilda from Katherine's lap. "Oh, all right. You can come with us, Mom, but only if you promise you won't say Santa's not real anymore. Okay?"

"You're in no position to bargain—"

"*Jet Jupiter to the rescue!*" From under the table, an action-adventure hero leaped to his feet...and banged his head on the underside of the table.

"Owwww-oh!" Andy yelled and began to cry... loudly and in great, gulping sobs.

"Andy!" Abby jumped to her feet in sympathy... and began jumping up and down on the couch, because the opportunity was there.

Katherine's heart jerked with maternal alarm, and she would have jumped up, but couldn't easily get her feet disentangled from the robe. By the time she managed to put her feet firmly on the floor, Gabe was already kneeling next to her son, roughing his hair with a gentle hand, checking for injury while distracting him with a soothing, "You've got to remember to wear your helmet, Jet. And it's always a good idea to open the hatch of your rocket ship before you eject."

It was exactly what Katherine would have done. Well, maybe she would have given him a kiss and a slight scolding for hiding under the table in the first place, but essentially, it would have accomplished the same results. But here was this man, uninvited, taking over her role... and all she could manage to feel, above her pounding heartbeat, was relief. "Are you all right?" she asked, falling back on the standard question of mothers everywhere, regardless of situation.

Andy rubbed his head, blinked back his tears, and ignored her in favor of Gabe. "I don't have a helmet," he said with a sniffle.

"What do you mean, you don't have a helmet?" Gabe looked appropriately astonished. "Well, we'll just fix that right now. Come with me." Taking Andy's hand, he led the way to the kitchen.

Curious, and not a little protective, Katherine followed, pausing only long enough to grab Abby on one of her gymnastic maneuvers, thereby saving the sofa from imminent destruction. She stopped in the kitchen doorway, unwilling to wedge into the small space Gabe again occupied with such presence. She watched as he opened first one cabinet door and then another. "Does he need an ice pack?" she asked, suddenly concerned that Andy's bump on the head was worse than she'd thought. A concussion, maybe.

"He needs a helmet." Gabe pulled out a large saucepan, gauged the measurements in a glance and, with a nod, placed the aluminum pan over Andy's red curls. "There, now we just need a chin strap...." Reaching up, he removed his tie and, with a few twists and a couple of knots, Andy's saucepan helmet was secured on his happy little head.

"Hey, cool." Andy stroked the chin strap and patted the top of the pan, and then, all smiles, he looked up at Katherine. "How does it look, Mom?"

"Very handsome," she said, her smile wrapped in a heartful of love. "Jet Jupiter never looked better."

"You look really stupid," Abby told him. "And you can't wear a dumb helmet when we go looking for Santa Claus. Can he, Gabe?"

Gabe held up his thumb and sighted Abby from ear to ear. "I think you could wear something a little less bulky." He lifted a plastic bowl from the shelf and settled it...with great care and fussing...on her head. "What do you think?" he asked. "There's one other possibility, but it's blue."

Katherine thought Abby would have nothing to do

with wearing a bowl on her head, even if it was a pretend helmet, but she made a couple of adjustments on either side and said, "I like yellow best. But what about my chin strap?"

Gabe frowned, then looked at Katherine. "Give me your sash."

"I don't think so." She covered the sailor's knot at her waist defensively.

"Oh, for Pete's sake, Mom." Abby pushed Katherine's hand aside and set to work untying the knot. "I just want to *borrow* it."

Katherine felt a flush creep onto her cheeks, but whether it was because the kitchen seemed so *cozy* all of a sudden or because Gabe had asked her to take off her belt, she couldn't determine. As if she would blush over anything so silly. Realizing with a start that she was not only blushing, but staring into Gabe's attractive brown eyes while she did it, she bent her head and tried to speed up her daughter's fumbling attempt to undo the knot. "Do you want me to do it?" she asked.

"No, I can." The tip of Abby's tongue appeared between her lips as she struggled persistently with the belt.

Katherine shifted her weight from one bare foot to the other and waited for what seemed like eons before the belt fell from around her waist and was caught in Gabe's big hand. With a sigh, she clutched the lapels of her robe and whirled out of the kitchen like a storm cloud in search of a lightning rod. She was outwardly serene and unbothered when Abby raced up to her a minute later, all decked out in a yellow plastic bowl secured on her head with a white terry-cloth sash, which wrapped twice over the top of her "helmet" and was tied dashingly under her chin. "Look, Mom. Gabe made me a helmet, too. Now, I'm Barbie Jupiter."

"Girls can't be laser rangers," Andy informed her, leveling his laser gun at her helmet. "You can be a cheerleader."

"I don't *wanta* be a cheerleader! I can, too, be a laser ranger, can't I, Mom?"

"Yes, you may." Katherine picked up Gabe's overcoat and offered it to him, along with an expectant look and a step toward the front door. "This could get nasty," she said. "You'll want to leave before there's any bloodshed."

Gabe hesitated, standing next to the dining room table, looking so very comfortable in her home that she felt a renewed sense of urgency to get him out. "Will you let me take them to Macy's this afternoon?" he asked.

"Macy's?" she repeated, surprised by both the idea and the destination.

"Macy's?" Andy stopped laser activity long enough to repeat the magic word. "Are we going to Macy's?"

Abby butted Andy's arm with her helmeted head. "Me and Gabe are going," she informed him. "You have to stay home with Mom."

Katherine ignored them, hoping to postpone the inevitable argument. "I'm sorry," she said, politely but firmly. "I don't know you well enough to let you take the twins anywhere."

"Then come with us."

"And look for Santa Claus?" She shook her head. "That would be a waste of time, now wouldn't it?"

"It wouldn't, Mom!" Andy grabbed her hand in a tight plea. "Just 'cause you don't believe doesn't mean me and Abby can't. Please, Mom? Please, let us go see Santa Claus at Macy's. Please? Please? Please?"

"We want to really, really bad, Mom." Abby added, making a readjustment to her bathrobe belt bow.

Katherine looked at Gabe, frowning, wondering why he hadn't let the twins' interest in detectives die a natural death. Didn't he know that the object of a child's curiosity changed at least a hundred times a day? And she didn't believe for an instant that someone as sensible as she was could hold any interest at all for someone as frivolous as he obviously was. Slipping her finger in between Andy's hand and hers, she eased the pressure of his death grip. "I have always told you the truth," she told her son. "I've never lied to you," she turned to Abby. "And when I told you Santa Claus wasn't real, it was the truth. It still is."

"But, Mom, we need to find out for ourselves."

Gabe cleared his throat, and she shot him a warning glance, but he only shrugged. He probably knew that *she* knew Andy had her dead to rights. How many times had she told them to look up the answers to their questions in the encyclopedia? Or stood aside while they discovered for themselves how something was done? Whoever said "Out of the mouths of babes'' had probably been seven years old when he said it. Damn, damn, damn. She did not want to go to Macy's. She made one desperate attempt to salvage her afternoon and her steadfast belief in the value of telling the truth. "Wouldn't you rather go to the museum? You're going to be disappointed when you see Santa Claus and realize he's a fake."

"No, we won't," Andy was quick to assure her. "We won't be disappointed, Mom, I promise."

"Gabe won't take us to see a fake Santa 'cause we gave him all our money to find the real one." Abby's smile was beautiful to behold, and Katherine was glad to see that Gabe got the full impact of it. He shifted under the deluge of childish trust, and Katherine began to feel better about the change in her plans. Why not let him take the twins to *see* good old Santa Claus? Let him find out for himself that it didn't pay to take money from children on the pretext that he could deliver magic. And she'd go along, just to watch him squirm.

"All right, then," she said, dazzling Gabe with a smile of her own. "Macy's, it is."

The response was deafening, as the children bounced around the room like grasshoppers in homemade helmets. "Macy's! Macy's!" they chanted. "We get to go to Macy's!"

Gabe watched them with a smile that Katherine thought looked the tiniest bit apprehensive. She wanted to lean close to his ear and whisper, *"Be afraid. Be very afraid."* But, like the twins, he needed to find out some things for himself.

Chapter Four

"I have to go to the bathroom."

"Again?" Gabe looked suspiciously at the freckled face looking up at him. "Are you sure?"

"Of course he's sure." Katherine's voice added a certain snap to the confirmation, and the way she grabbed Andy's hand left no doubt that she believed her son...or that she was grasping at any opportunity to get out of the line of children and parents who were waiting to see Santa Claus. From where he stood on Macy's Bridge to Santa's House, Gabe couldn't see anything except harried parents, tired children, and an occasional glimpse of a cheerful Macy's employee dressed in an elf suit. "I'll take him this time," Katherine said, her tone brooking no argument. "Do you have to go, Abby?"

"Nope." Abby's feet swung in loose circles while she hung over the wooden railing like limp spaghetti. "I don't need to go."

"You can't take me, Mom." Andy informed her importantly. "Because I have to go to the *guys'* bathroom, not the *girls'* bathroom."

"I've been taking you to the *ladies'* bathroom ever

since you were born and you never complained before.''

"But, Mom, I'm *not* a lady, and it's embracing to go in there.''

Katherine frowned. "Embarrassing?''

"Yeah.'' Andy nodded vigorously. "That. And Gabe can take me to the guys' bathroom, Mom, 'cause he's a guy, and he doesn't mind, do ya, Gabe?''

With a sigh, Katherine lifted her gray eyes imploringly to Gabe's. "I don't suppose you'd—''

"Mind?'' Gabe supplied, knowing that wasn't what she'd been about to say at all. She'd been about to ask him if he'd please take them all out of this line, off the Bridge to Santa's House and away from the cacophony of kids crying, whining, stomping, and making every other kind of noise known to kidkind. If he'd been in her place, that was certainly what he would have asked...and long before now, too. "Of course I don't mind taking him to the *guys'* bathroom,'' he said magnanimously. "I think there's plenty of time to go and get back before it's our turn to see Santa.''

Her gaze trailed to the brick chimney that, from where they stood, was all that could be seen of Santa's House. "Plenty of time,'' she repeated dismally.

Gabe took Andy's hand. "Come on, kiddo, let's go.''

He could feel the heat of Katherine's resentful gaze on the back of his neck as he excused his and Andy's way to the end of the line, and momentary freedom. "I did it real good that time, didn't I, Gabe?" Andy's gap-toothed grin flashed satisfaction. "I said it just like you told me, didn't I? Mom never even figured it out I was just p'tending I needed to go to the bathroom." He gave a little skip. "Can we get another hot chocolate?"

"Any more hot chocolate and you *will* need a bathroom." Gabe held on to Andy's hand protectively as they escaped the section of the eighth floor that housed Santa's House. Okay, so it was a cheap trick, but he clearly wasn't cut out for this Christmas ritual of waiting to see Santa Claus. Even if it had been his idea. Even if he'd insisted on coming.

He'd thought Katherine seemed oddly congenial, if not a little smug, when they all left her apartment nearly...he checked his watch...three hours ago. She wasn't feeling particularly congenial anymore. She was tired, cranky, and nearly as sick of the whole idea as he was himself. He did feel guilty for leaving her behind to wait with Abby...again. But when a boy had to go, he had to go. And right now, he and Andy had to go somewhere away from that line of people.

It wasn't as if Katherine hadn't gotten to step out of line a couple of times, herself. Once when Abby decided to skip all the turns and switchbacks in the bridge to Santa's House and go directly to the front of the line. And once more, when the twins slipped under the railing and helped themselves to some toys in the Elves' Workshop display.

If he'd had any idea they wouldn't be able to walk right up, sit on Santa's lap and ask for a gazillion toys, he never would have suggested the visit. Although he had to admit that watching Katherine had made the wait almost bearable. Balancing the cool responses she made to his attempts at conversation against the not-at-all-cool blushes that randomly invaded her cheeks had provided a world of intrigue in itself. Trying to catch the tail end of a fleeting déjà vu and figuring out why, at moments, she seemed so damned familiar had occupied a good chunk of his attention, as well.

But after standing next to her for the better part of the afternoon, he found her more of a mystery than before. She had made no secret of her impatience with the whole Santa setup at Macy's, but she'd demonstrated tremendous patience with the twins during the wait. Gabe admired her for letting her kids discover their own truths, despite her personal distaste for this particular quest. And while she might not be crazy about having him around, she was willing to give him the benefit of the doubt because, whatever their reasons, her children liked him.

"I got an idea, Gabe." Andy tugged on his hand. "We can do our Christmas shopping."

"What?" Gabe asked in pretended alarm. "Do my shopping before Christmas Eve? You can't be serious."

"I am," Andy assured him with very serious blue eyes. "Come on. I'll buy somethin' for you and you can buy somethin' for me."

"But then you won't be surprised when you open the present on Christmas," said Gabe, who until that moment had had no thought of buying presents for anyone other than Gun and Louisa.

"Yes, I will." Andy pulled him toward the action-adventure toys, which were conveniently displayed at child's-eye-level near the center aisle. "I'll be s'prised 'cause that present will be a secret. This present won't. It'll be 'cause I've been so good at waitin' to see Santa Claus."

There might have been the threat of blackmail in that statement, but Gabe opted to believe it was just innocent excitement. Which had to be the reason he allowed himself to be pulled down the aisle toward Jet Jupiter's assorted accessories...wondering all the way why he'd never known before how persuasive little boys could be.

KATHERINE HADN'T BEEN quite eight years old the last time she'd stepped through the Thirty-fourth Street entrance and into the mercantile world of Macy's department store. It had seemed bigger back then, and so glamorous that she hadn't been able to contain her excitement. Her mother had practically had to drag her through the aisles and up the escalators, warning her not to dawdle and scolding her for not watching where she was going. Which seemed odd, because she could remember distinctly trying to look everywhere, see everything, and absorb the experience that was Macy's at Christmastime. Funny. She hadn't thought about that in years. But then, she hadn't been in Macy's in years, either. Small wonder, then, to find the memories returning with her.

"How much longer till we see Santa Claus?" Abby asked, her voice growing perceptibly more impatient.

"Santa Claus?" Katherine lowered her eyebrows in a perplexed frown. "Do you mean, how much longer until we see the *man* the store *hired* to put on a costume and ask children what they want for Christmas?"

"Mommmmm..." Abby drew the single syllable into a long humming whine. "You promised you wouldn't say stuff like that today, 'member?"

"If I'd known this excursion was going to take all afternoon, I wouldn't have promised anything of the sort," she said. "And, frankly, after standing in this line for this long, I think I deserve to feel just a little out of sorts, don't you?"

"You shoulda stayed at home. Then me and Andy and Gabe coulda had fun." Abby kicked the rail support a couple of times, making a dull thudding noise. "I shoulda gone to the bathroom with them."

Me too, Katherine thought, wishing she could be anywhere but here. "They should be back any minute, now. Then you and I can go."

Abby offered a skeptical glance. "I don't want to go until I've seen Santa Claus."

"We'll be back before it's your turn."

"No, we won't. You won't bring me back in time to see him."

"Of course I will, Abby. Why would you think that I wouldn't?"

"'Cause you don't like Santa Claus and you don't

like Gabe and you don't want me to like them, neither.''

"Either. And that isn't true.'' The denial lacked
conviction, though, and Katherine tried harder.
"Well, okay, I don't like this Santa stuff, and I'm
not as charmed by Gabe as you and Andy are, but I
don't dislike him.''

"Yes, you do,'' Abby said, with a few more well-
aimed kicks at the support. "I think he's funny, but
you don't. You don't laugh at his jokes.''

Katherine racked her brain to recall any humor in
this long afternoon, but the only joke she could appreciate was the one on her...the one in which she'd
agreed to this entire ill-fated trip. Well, she had a
few choice words for the man in the Santa suit—if
she ever saw him. And a few more for Gabe Housley...when he finally returned with her son.

The thought had barely skated past when she heard
his voice behind her in line, recognizable over all the
other voices around her. "Excuse us,'' he was saying, his tone one of pleasant confidence that he
wasn't, really, inconveniencing anyone. "Thank you.
Sorry. Excuse the kid, please. He's a little excited.
Too much hot chocolate. Excuse me. Sorry.''

A pause, then Andy's voice above the rest, "Hey,
there's Mom. We're back, Mom! Abby! Hey, Abby!
Look at the cool present Gabe bought me!''

Katherine's head turned nearly as fast as Abby's
did. *Present?* she thought. Did the man have no sense
whatsoever?

"Present?'' Abby echoed aloud. "Andy got a
present?''

Then the guys were back, all smiles and relaxed good humor. Andy, full of importance, showed Abby his toy. "Don't touch it," he warned.

"Did you miss us?" Gabe asked Katherine.

"You bet. Abby and I were just talking about how dull the last *hour* has been without you."

"As opposed to the lively hour before that?" His lips formed that irritating half smile. "And we weren't gone an hour. Forty-five minutes, maybe. Forty-six, tops. This is Christmas, you know. The store's crowded. Besides, it's your turn, now. You and Abby can stretch your legs and do a little shopping, if you want, while Andy and I hold our place in line."

"Believe it or not, I don't think we have time to go and get back. The line actually seems to be moving."

He craned his neck to see over the tops of several dozen heads in front of them. "By golly, I think you're right. There may actually *be* a Santa Claus at the end of this line."

"For your sake, I hope so. He'd better be the one-and-only *real* Santa, too, because otherwise you're going to have a mutiny on your hands."

"You're counting on that, aren't you, Kate? Don't bother to deny it. I hear that smug confidence in your voice. But everyone knows the real Santa Claus can be found at Macy's and, in a few minutes, when you see old Kris Kringle work his magic on the twins, you're going to be sorry you doubted me."

"Really? Well, to be honest, I find your faith in

Macy's rather touching. Naive, but touching. However, I think you have bigger problems."

"What? You're not going to stand there and tell me you think I can't find the Easter Bunny at Bloomingdale's, are you?"

She almost felt sorry for him. Almost. "No, this problem is a little more immediate. It's Abby."

"Abby?" he repeated, his gaze dropping to her bent red head. "She seems fine to me. She hasn't changed her mind about wanting to see Santa, has she?"

"I don't think so, but you're going to find out right about..." Katherine paused, waiting for the telltale signs of impending disaster.

"*Don't* touch it, Abby." Andy jerked the toy out of his sister's reach. "Gabe bought it for *me*."

"...now." Katherine concluded, just as Abby turned angry blue eyes upward, looking to the adults for justice.

"Andy won't share." Each word held its own world of outrage, but the complaint was quickly followed by a cagey and somewhat winsome batting of the eyelashes. "Did you get *me* a present, Gabe?"

Katherine knew it was her duty to jump right in—Mother Manners to the rescue—and remind Abby that it was impolite to ask for gifts. But noting how startled, chagrined and helpless Gabe looked, she decided a mother couldn't be expected to correct every single etiquette violation.

Gabe turned to Katherine, clearly hoping for assistance. "I thought I'd take her to the toy department after we've seen Santa Claus."

Katherine couldn't keep amusement from lending a curve to her lips. "Well," she said, "think again."

Abby put one hand on her hip. "You did bring me a present, didn't you, Gabe?"

He stooped to her level to facilitate an explanation, a move Katherine deemed thoughtful, but not child-proof. "No, Abby," he said. "I figured you'd want to pick it out yourself."

"I do," she said. "Let's go."

"We can't go now," Gabe explained. "We wouldn't get back in time to see Santa Claus."

With a glance at the long line, which extended as far as she could see, Abby assessed the possibility and made her choice in the blink of an eye. "I don't want to see Santa. I want to go get a toy."

Gabe reasoned with her. "But we've waited all this time just to see Santa."

"I want to go get my toy."

The quirk on his lips became a little less smile and a little more frown. "If we get out of line now, Abby, we won't get to see Santa. We'll miss our turn."

"I don't care." She crossed her arms, obstinacy anchored in every move she made. "He's not the *real* Santa Claus, anyway."

That's my girl, Katherine thought, her own gaze shifting to Gabe to gauge his reaction.

"He *might* be," Gabe countered a bit tersely. "And if we get out of line now, we'll never know."

"*I'm* not gettin' out of line." Andy upped the pressure with his unsolicited opinion. "*I'm* gonna see Santa Claus."

"We're all going to see Santa." Gabe straightened, lending authority to his statement. "First we'll see Santa and tell him what we want for Christmas, *then* we'll do some more shopping."

Abby's pout was a work of art. The tears welling in her eyes were shining stars of accusation. The trembling of her lower lip was poetry in motion. Her half sniffle, half sigh was a masterpiece of manipulation. Katherine had a low tolerance for pouting, but she was never unmoved by Abby's mastery of it. And she knew without looking at him that Gabe would crumble before it like the walls of Jericho in the wake of Joshua's trumpet. He would buckle and take Abby to the toy department, leaving Katherine to shepherd Andy through Santa's House—something she wanted to do almost as badly as she wanted to get a nose ring. Then, afterward, Andy would tell Abby how cool Santa had been and how she should have been there to tell him all the toys *she* wanted for Christmas, which meant Abby would demand they get *back* in line, so she, too, could have the wondrous experience. Andy would pout if they did. Abby would pout if they didn't, and Katherine would end up being the mean old mother, no matter how soon she managed to intervene and settle the question. The scenario was as clear as glass in her mind, and she wished Gabe could do something to prevent it...which was only slightly less likely than her being able to do so.

But, to her surprise, Gabe took one good look at the da Vinci of pouters and stooped to Abby's level once more. "Excuse me, Miss Harmon," he said. "But there's something on your nose."

Abby sniffed. "What?"

"A freckle named Frances."

She blinked. "There is not."

"I don't like to contradict a lady, but there most certainly is." He tapped the side of her nose. "It's definitely Frances, the fretful freckle. I haven't seen another freckle like it since my cousin sneezed so hard, he blew Frances right off his nose."

The shimmer of tears was history, the trembling lip naught but a memory, the toy controversy temporarily on hold. "That's silly. You can't sneeze off a freckle."

"I can," Andy announced, and demonstrated with several exaggerated snorts. "There. Did I do it, Gabe? Look at my nose."

"He's lookin' at *my* nose." Abby elbowed Andy to keep him from stepping into her spotlight. "Go play with your stupid Jet Jupiter rocket ship."

Katherine looked on in awe and annoyance. She never could think fast enough to divert Abby's pout or Andy's charge-ahead stubbornness. But Gabe, a virtual stranger, had seemed to do it effortlessly, averting a scene and sidetracking a battle of wills. Not only that, he was getting what he wanted...peace while they finished waiting to see Santa. She didn't understand it, and although she knew she probably ought to be grateful, she wasn't.

The line moved forward, and on the other side of the switchback, Santa's House was suddenly in view. If there was an inch of plywood not covered in candy canes and other assorted plastic goodies, Katherine couldn't imagine where it might be. The twins' mouths fell open in awed delight. "Look, Mom. It's Santa's House," they said, so nearly in unison it was hard to know which child had said what.

"Ah, finally, our destination...the North Pole and the one-and-only real Macy's department store Santa Claus." Gabe's voice was so close to her ear, she couldn't tell if he startled her or if the warmth of his breath caused a chain reaction of awareness along her spine. "Sorry," he said. "I didn't mean to startle you."

"You didn't," came her instant, untruthful reply. "I was just a little unnerved by the sight of so much 'sweetness' in one place. Who do you suppose designed this Nightmare on Gingerbread Alley?"

"Someone who is undoubtedly proud to have given such unmitigated delight to the thousands of children—and adults—who believe it's okay to be a kid at Christmas." His voice was no longer close...or warm...and Katherine was sorry she'd let his unsettling nearness prompt her into making a cynical and unkind remark. On the other hand, this was not *her* idea of unmitigated delight.

"Look, Mom." Andy tugged on her little finger, urging her toward the rail.

"Look, Mom." Abby pointed, excitedly. "It's just like the gingerbread house in the magazine, the one you can make at home."

Then again—on the other hand—delight often found her completely by surprise. She felt Gabe's frown center on the back of her neck and gave herself permission to ignore him. After all, she'd known going into this that she wasn't exactly on his agenda of delights, either.

A door in Santa's House opened, and a couple of leggy elves came out to work the line, handing out coloring books, crayons and party whistles, the paper kind that unfurled with a low trill when blown. "Got your list ready for Santa?" one of the elves asked. "Have you been naughty or nice?" asked the other.

As if by magic, the long, impatient wait was forgotten. Children laughed and parents smiled as they pointed out the jingling bells on the elves' hats and on their curly-topped shoes. Andy and Abby hung over the railing, their attention secured, their eyes wide with curiosity as the elves came closer. Andy stopped watching their progress only long enough to glance over his shoulder. "Hey, Gabe, look! It's Santa's elves." He pointed to the nearest one...the one with pretty, dark eyes...the one whose costume did nothing to disguise her lushly feminine shape. "What's her name?"

"Sheila." Gabe supplied readily, and the elf turned in their direction.

"Hey, ya, Gabe!" she said, her flashing smile indicating not only that she recognized him, but that she had a darn good idea of where he stood on the nice-or-naughty scale, as well. "Merry Christmas!"

Katherine looked at him with interest. "You know an elf?"

"He knows all the elves, Mom." Abby used the railing like a balance beam, levering her body weight so that she could lean out for a better view. "He knows their names and everything."

"All the elves?" Katherine repeated with droll humor. "Names and everything?"

He shrugged with undue modesty. "I studied elf culture in college. Aced the class."

"I'll bet she was your instructor, too."

"Sheila? Nah."

At the repetition of her name, the shapely elf winked seductively and waved. "I'll be right there," she called. "Don't go away."

Palm out, Gabe curled his fingers in a reply that seemed not only reticent, but bashful, as well. "This may surprise you," he said in an undertone. "But she's not a real elf."

"Noooo..." Katherine drew the syllable out in exaggerated surprise. "You don't mean she's an... *impostor?*"

"Ssshhhh, you don't want to blow her cover."

"So...she's working as an undercover elf?" Katherine leaned closer to whisper, "Isn't she a little, uh, tall for that?"

He slanted an appreciative glance at the luscious Sheila, who was passing out crayons and coloring books with unelflike haste. "She's five-eight, a hundred and thirty-one pounds, twenty-one years old and twenty-one inches around the waist. Her other measurements are equally impressive, and she is—in her own words—*well-rounded*. She plans to become a photojournalist and wants to help bring about world peace in her lifetime." Catching Katherine's astonished gaze, he lifted his shoulders in a guileless shrug. "She's plays a mean hand of five-card Stud, too."

Katherine couldn't have been more astounded if he suddenly poked her in the eye. "If you get that kind of information from those monthly poker games, someone needs to notify the authorities."

The corners of his mouth lifted in a grin. "I learned all I know about Sheila from the dossier she filled out for the Miss Staten Island pageant. She was a contestant. I was a judge. There, you see, I came by the information quite innocently."

"I suppose there's a perfectly innocent reason why you remember her statistics, too."

"I have an excellent memory," he stated flatly...and Katherine suddenly wanted to poke *him* in the eye. If he said he never forgot a pretty face, damn it, she would.

"So do you remember all the contestants' facts and *figures,* or just the ones who went on to become Santa's elves?"

"You're taking this a bit personally, aren't you, Kate?"

"No," she snapped. "I'm not. And don't call me Kate."

"Katherine."

She didn't like that any better. "Just don't talk to me."

She could feel his questioning gaze as she stooped beside the twins and watched them watch the approaching elves. "I wonder why those women are wearing elf costumes," she said, as if it was a question that truly puzzled her. "Do you suppose they're getting *paid* to do it?"

"You're doin' it again, Mom," Abby warned. "And you promised you wouldn't."

"Yeah," Andy agreed. "You promised."

Katherine sighed and rose to her feet, again. She was going to have to decide which was worse...the twins acting like normal kids—even if it wasn't the way they normally acted—or her own embarrassing overreaction every time Gabe said two words she could conceivably interpret as a reference to the kiss he did not remember. She risked a glance at him and found him watching her cautiously...sort of like a backpacker who suddenly finds himself face-to-face with a bear.

"Look, Gabe," she said over a tight knot of resistance in her throat. "I'm sorry if I seem a little tense. It's been a long afternoon, and..."

"Hello there!" Sheila arrived at their section of the bridge, shoved goody bags over the railing without paying much attention to which outstretched hands claimed them, and smiled at Gabe as if he had single-handedly crowned her queen of the elves. "I never expected to see you here," she said eagerly. "I didn't think you had any kids."

"I borrowed these so I'd have an excuse to spend the afternoon at Macy's."

"That's so sweet." Sheila's laugh was high-pitched, and much too enthusiastic for minimum wage. "I've called your office dozens of times, but you were always in a meeting. I was beginning to think you were avoiding me, but now here you are."

"We're here to see Santa." The words rushed out, making Gabe's voice sound vaguely uncomfortable to Katherine's untrained ear, but then, she wasn't exactly skilled in the nuances of flirtation. "The twins…" he continued, placing a hand affectionately on each of the children. "…wanted to give Santa their Christmas list, so here we are. That's why we're here. To see Santa."

"They're here to see Santa," Katherine corrected. "I'm here as the token parent."

Sheila's gaze switched to Katherine, assessed and dismissed her in the blink of an eye, and returned full strength to Gabe. "I get off in another hour. Why don't you pick me up after you are, uh, through with the kiddies, and we'll catch up on where you've been and what I've been doing since the pageant. I've been hoping I'd get the chance to spend some time with you, so this must be fate, huh?"

She all but purred the invitation, and Katherine wondered if it was hard to learn how to do that. "Sheila?" she said politely. "Could you tell me how to make that sound? That throaty thing you just did? I've never had an occasion that called for purring, but I'd like to be prepared, just in case."

"Excuse me?"

Icicles could have formed on Sheila's words, but Katherine prevented frostbite with a warm smile. "I'm sorry. I interrupted, didn't I? Excuse me. I'll just watch the *kiddies* while you talk to Gabe. Maybe I can pick up your technique by listening."

Sheila stared hard at Katherine before giving Gabe a what-are-you-doing-with-her-anyway? arch of the eyebrows. "So, can you make it?" She glanced at her watch. "I get to shed this costume in fifty-two minutes. Just tell me where to meet you."

Gabe rubbed the back of his neck. "The North Pole?"

"You're such a tease." Sheila patted his cheek. "How about the Thirty-fourth Street entrance in an hour?"

"I don't think that's a good—"

"Hey," Abby said, interrupting her. "You're not a *real* elf. Real elves don't paint their fingernails."

Sheila spared a glance—no more—for Abby before she shoved a second goody bag into the child's hands and returned to her main objective. "Don't say no," she told Gabe. "You can change your plans for me, can't you? Just this once?"

There could have been a voice lesson in there somewhere, but Katherine was distracted by the sight of Andy kneeling on the bridge and trying his seven-year-old best to look up Sheila's little green skirt. "Andy!" She whispered his name out of the side of her mouth as she reached down—trying desperately to seem casual—and tapped him on the shoulder. He pushed her hand away and renewed his efforts. "Andy!" This time she made the whisper a little louder and the tap more definite.

"Wait a minute, Mom," her budding lothario said loudly. "I got to see what color underwear she's got on!"

As moments go, Katherine had had better. Even in the noisy room, Andy's voice carried and in the hush that followed, Katherine half expected to hear someone shout, *"Grenade!"* and to see everyone dive for cover. But Sheila was the only one to shout, and *"Grenade!"* wasn't exactly what she said.

"Ommm!" Abby clapped her hand over her mouth...but only for an instant. "You said a bad word. That *proves* you're not a real elf."

"She's not wearin' green underwear, neither." Andy confirmed, dusting his hands as he got off his knees. "Gabe said elves always wear green."

"You little demon!" Sheila reached for Andy. Katherine reached for Sheila. Gabe was quicker, pulling Andy out of the way and stopping any further unelflike comments with a gruff "Don't even think about touching him, unless you want to tangle with me first."

Sheila backed off, blinking her pretty eyes in angry surprise. "I thought he wasn't your kid."

"He is today." Gabe sounded stern, protective, and ready to take on an entire army of pushy women. "Now, why don't you go back to work before I decide to report you to the big guy himself."

Sheila lifted one shoulder in an unrepentant shrug. "Mr. Macy died years ago."

"Well, Santa Claus didn't," Gabe answered. "And since we're on the subject, there's no reason for you to keep calling my office, Sheila. It's a waste of your time and mine."

"Well..." Reshuffling the goody bags on her arm, Sheila tossed her gleaming dark hair and jingled the bell on her hat. "That, of course, is your loss. But don't think I'll forget this when I become a celebrity. I won't be calling Housley Security then. Make no mistake about it. When I'm a star—"

"Hey! Elf-lady! My kid wants a coloring book!" From down the line, the voice of a tired and exasperated father called for help. "Could you stop talking and bring him one before I go stark raving *crazy?*"

Katherine silently thanked the man, his son, and the stern-looking elf who had stepped around the side of Santa's House to see what was going on. Sheila didn't wait for marching orders from headquarters. She began handing out goody bags with a vengeance...and a smile, however insincere.

Katherine turned with a sigh of relief...at the same exact instant Gabe turned...and sighed with relief. Their eyes met, and for just a moment, she felt a bond, a mutual purpose. The same sort of commonality she imagined a woman would share with the father of her children. But then she blinked, and it was gone.

Gabe ruffled Andy's curly hair. "I thought you were going to get us kicked out of line, buddy."

Andy's grin flashed no hint of remorse. "I had to find out if she was a real elf or not."

"Couldn't you have checked her ears?" Gabe asked. "Looking under skirts is just not something gentlemen do."

Andy frowned. "What about guys? Do *they* look?"

Gabe hesitated, and Katherine jumped in to provide the definitive "No," and a distracting "What's in the bag?"

Abby was first to thrust her hand into the plastic sack, but Andy came up first with the main prize, and half a second later, they were zestfully blowing the whistles at, and into, each other's faces.

"I'm sorry about that," Gabe said. "I knew she was pushy, but I didn't think she'd be rude." He looked over Katherine's head, presumably at the retreating Sheila, and then his brown eyes came back to apologize again. "I'm not sure, but I think that *she* thinks I'm going to get her a job as Michael Bolton's bodyguard. It's the only reason I can think of for her to have singled me out from all the other judges."

Katherine looked at him, at the appealing line of his mouth, at the feathery laugh lines around his eyes, at the strong angle of his jaw, at the firm character of his chin, at the hair that drooped onto his forehead, and wondered if he was really that unaware of his own sex appeal. "If I thought you could get me close to Michael Bolton's body, I'd single you out myself."

His eyebrows rose. "Katherine. I'm surprised at you. And just as I was getting the message that you're not much interested in men."

"Just because I don't know how to *purr* when I talk doesn't mean I'm not interested in men. I'm particular, that's all. Very particular."

"Okay, I'll bite. What kind of man…in particular…interests you?"

"The kind who remembers—" She snapped her lips shut before the rest of that sentence could see daylight. The line moved forward, and Katherine gratefully moved with it.

Gabe moved, too, and when they stopped, he was

even closer to her than before. "The kind of man who remembers...what?"

"Nothing." She pretended a preoccupation with counting the dwindling number of people in front of them. "We're almost at Santa's House," she announced, although the twins weren't listening and Gabe wasn't going to be distracted.

"There is something going on here," he said, almost as if he were talking to himself. "I know this sounds like a line, but I can't shake this feeling that you and I have some sort of history together, that there's something I ought to remember. Is it possible that...? Is there any chance that you and I...?"

His voice trailed off, and Katherine closed her eyes, willing him not to recall, yet hoping, for some unfathomable and stupid reason, that he would. Then, to her utter horror, she heard her own voice supplying the answer before he had half a chance to complete the question. "Okay. It was a kiss. We kissed under the mistletoe in your office last Christmas Eve. I hardly remember the incident, myself, and it was obvious you'd forgotten all about it, so I wasn't going to say anything. I mean, it wasn't as if it meant anything to either one of us. It was simply a case of mistaken identity on your part...a little too much Christmas spirit on mine. So there, now you know, and we can both forget all about it again."

"We kissed?" He sounded unflatteringly astonished. "You and me?"

"I," she corrected with a sigh. "You and I, and yes, we did."

"Kissed?" he repeated, as if he had to be sure that

was what she'd said. "I thought maybe we'd gone to school together and I used to pull your pigtails or something, but..." His voice faded away. "I kissed you? How could I have forgotten that?"

All too easily, Katherine wanted to say. "There's no reason you should have remembered" was what she said, instead. "I'm sure I would have forgotten it, myself, if..." She couldn't think of a single reason she hadn't forgotten, other than that, for her, it hadn't been any ordinary kiss...it had been a kick-off-the shoes, curl-the-toes, knock-the-socks-off kiss. A Christmas Eve kiss, full of mystery and magic and exciting anticipation. Even factoring in the sad reality that it had been the only kiss of the entire year for her and the only memorable one for several years before that, she couldn't rate it as anything less than unforgettable. She sighed again. "It was just a kiss. Forget it."

"Not in this lifetime," he said. "Definitely not until I know how it happened."

"I'd rather not talk about this anymore."

"I'm afraid it's too late for that option. You can't drop something like that into the conversation and then say you don't want to talk about it. Come on, Kate. Tell me what happened."

She could not believe she'd opened herself up for this. If she'd just kept her mouth shut... "It was Christmas Eve. You closed the building early for a private party. I worked until late afternoon, and when I went to leave, I was locked in and the security guard wasn't at his desk in the lobby, so I went to your office looking for him. The lights went out. We bumped into each other in the dark. You said something about the damn mistletoe, and you kissed me. There, see? I told you it was nothing.''

"Wait a minute. I do remember the party and that somebody turned out the lights.'' He paused, obviously searching his memory for further details. ''Are you positive it was me?''

It wasn't enough that he couldn't remember, he wanted to make absolutely certain she knew he couldn't remember. ''Yes,'' she said, thinking that if her blush got any brighter, Santa would be trying to hire her to help Rudolph light the way. ''It was you. It was me. Now, could we please change the subject?''

"You kissed me,'' Gabe said. ''I'll be damned.''

"Please, sir, lower your voice.'' An elf—the stern-faced senior male elf, whose name tag boasted that he was Macy's main elf—tapped him on the arm with a large candy cane. ''There are children present.''

"Sorry,'' Gabe said and turned again to Katherine. ''Had I been drinking?'' he asked, adding insult to injury. ''There was some killer eggnog at that party, as I recall.''

The elf scolded Gabe with a click of his tongue. ''You shouldn't talk that way in front of the children. If you're not careful, I'll have to write in 'naughty' beside your name.''

"He's not naughty.'' Abby stopped trying to see around the rather large derriere of the woman in front of her and came to Gabe's defense. ''And you'd better be nice to him, cuz he's a *real* Jack Kass.''

The man's mouth fell open. "Oh, my! Now, that kind of language just won't do. What if Santa had heard you say that?"

"He's not the *real* Santa Claus," Abby informed everyone within earshot...much to the elf's dismay. "He's just a man who was hired to dress up like Santa and listen to kids tell him what they want for Christmas."

"Yeah," Andy said. "Besides, there's nothin' wrong with sayin' Jack Kass. Our mom says it all the time."

The elf's stern expression swung to Katherine, and in the interest of getting out of Santa's House alive, Katherine clapped a hand each over Abby's and Andy's mouths and warned all of elfdom with a rush of tightly spoken threats. "They didn't say what you think they said, and even if they had, we've been waiting over three hours to see Santa and no one, not even Macy's main elf, is going to kick us out of line now. Understand?"

The elf eyed her, then rather ungraciously ushered them into the gingerbread house. Katherine had to duck to get under the candy-cane doorway, and Gabe had to practically double over to get inside. The room was small, stuffy, and sparsely furnished...which wouldn't have been all that bad if the furnishings hadn't been a large thronelike chair and if the person occupying the chair hadn't filled it to capacity. It could have been padding that rolled over his big black belt and pooched through the space between the chair arm and the chair seat. It could have been the costume that gave the area its musty mothball smell. But whatever the cause, the man at the center of the room—the Santa Claus they had been waiting such a long time to see—looked about as jovial as Katherine did.

She hoped, for the sake of the hundreds of kids still waiting in line, that this was just a temporary Claus, that the real Macy's Santa was on break and would be back in a few minutes. Because this man was so obviously a fake. From the top of his fusty red velvet hat to the visible string of elastic that held his false beard in place to the scuffed toes of his black boots—lace-ups!—he was a sorry excuse for the jolly old elf.

"Ho, ho, ho!" His monotone filled the room with uncomfortable, resonating vibrations. "What's your name, honey?" He motioned halfheartedly to Abby. "Come on over and talk to old Santa."

"I don't feel too good." Andy backed up, bumping into Katherine's knees. "I must've had too much hot chocolate. I think I'm gonna be sick."

Abby was pale, but she stood her ground, staring at the shabby, red-faced Santa with wide eyes.

"Ho, ho, ho," he repeated.

That was when Abby started screaming.

Chapter Five

There were three french fries left on the plate.

Gabe draped his arms across the back of the vinyl-covered booth and watched the stockpile dwindle to two as Abby captured the biggest fry between her thumb and forefinger. Fascinated, he counted to himself as she dipped her prize in the huge glob of ketchup on her plate—one, two, three dips, then a bite. One, two, three dips, and another bite. Always three dips...no more, no less...then the grand finish—a rhythmic lick of all fingers that had come into contact with either french fry or ketchup. It was the way she'd eaten every single bite of potato in her portion of the Monster Fries Plate, which was a specialty of the Sixth Avenue Diner, which was where he'd shepherded Katherine and the twins after their ignominious retreat from Santa's House.

His observation moved to Andy, who claimed the next fry, drowned it thoroughly in the lake of ketchup that had once been his plate, then inserted the fry into his mouth and pulled it slowly out again, removing the tomato coating in one efficient collaboration of mouth and vegetable. He then repeated the process until—as best Gabe could figure—the potato was finally so mushy it disintegrated in his mouth.

By default, the last french fry belonged to Katherine, but she took so long in reaching for it that the twins began eyeing it, and her, speculatively. One false move on her part, Gabe thought, and that fry was history. But just as Andy's hand inched forward, Katherine speared the fry with her fork, causing first Andy, then Abby, to sigh and kick back in the booth.

"I want a milk shake," Abby said.

"Me too." Andy smiled all around. "Strawberry."

"You cannot still be hungry. Not after the hamburgers you just put away." Katherine waved the fork and fry over the remains of the meal. Two pairs of blue eyes followed that french fry wherever it went.

"I am," Andy stated for a fact. "I'm still hungry."

"We are," Abby agreed. "We're hungry."

Katherine's eyes met Gabe's briefly, and he tried to hold her glance with a smile, but she quickly picked up the ketchup bottle and pointed it at Andy. "Are you *sure* you're feeling okay?" she asked.

Andy's gaze fell to the table, then swept back to his mother's with a glint of hope. "A milk shake would make my stomach feel a lot better."

"I don't think so. Not on top of everything else you've had to eat."

"But a milk shake would glue it all together, Mom," Abby explained solemnly. "Then he couldn't throw up any more."

"Yeah," Andy nodded a vigorous agreement. "I can't throw up if all the food's glued together. Ain't that right, Gabe?"

"*Isn't* that right," Katherine corrected.

"Makes perfect sense to me." Gabe smiled winsomely, ready for the annoyed glance he was sure was headed his way.

"No milk shakes," Katherine said, ignoring him in favor of the French fry, which she bit in two. "If you're thirsty, drink your water."

Andy's lower lip protruded, while Abby crawled up onto her knees and peered over the back of the booth behind them. "Hi," she said to the elderly couple who was sitting there. "Have you seen Santa Claus?" she asked. "I'm lookin' for him."

Gabe wondered if all seven-year-olds were this interesting, or if he was just in the mood for a double dose of unpredictable and fascinating behavior.

"We've already been to Macy's," Abby was continuing her one-sided conversation. "But don't take your kids there, because he's not the *real* Santa. The *real* Santa wouldn't have let that elf kick us out just cuz I screamed and my brother threw up."

Andy scrambled to his knees and joined her in conversing over the divider. "I'm the one that threw up," he announced proudly. "I drank too much hot chocolate. What are you drinkin'? Is that a milk shake? Is it strawberry?"

"Turn around," Katherine said, giving a tug to Abby's sleeve and tucking in one side of Andy's shirttail. "You're bothering those people."

"We're just talkin', Mom," Abby protested.

"You always tell us to be nice to old people."
Andy wiggled his shoulders, pulling the shirttail free
again. "We're just havin' good manners."

"It's rude to interrupt someone else's dinner. Now
turn around." Katherine smiled apologetically at
their nearest neighbors in the diner. "It's Christmas," she said, by way of explaining their behavior.
Then she breathed a tight-lipped command to the
twins. "Sit down!"

"Can we get a milk shake?"

"No. Sit. Now."

Abby dropped her fanny onto the bench seat with
a plop. "I'm thirsty," she said on a long and very
bored sigh.

"Drink your water."

Andy slid from a kneeling position into a slump.
"I don't drink water," he said. "Fish barf in it."

"That's why it's so good for you." Katherine
made a production out of scooting the glass in front
of her son. "Lots of vitamins and minerals."

"That's gross, Mom." Abby scooted the glass
back to the middle of the table, presumably so that
her brother wouldn't be tempted to drink fish barf.
"Why can't we have a milk shake? Gabe doesn't
mind, do ya, Gabe?"

"I mind," Katherine answered, before he could.
"And I'm your mother."

"But he's payin' for it," Abby said stubbornly.
"He said he would, didn't ya, Gabe?"

Gabe opened his mouth, only to hear Katherine
say, "But he isn't the one who's going to have to
get up with you in the middle of the night when your

stomach is upset and you're having nightmares, is he?''

Abby frowned, the wheels in her head spinning with the effort to get around that bit of mother logic.

Andy coated his finger in ketchup and popped it into his mouth. Then his eyes brightened and he pulled the finger out with a soft *schlupp* sound. "I got a great idea! Gabe can spend the night with us, and he can sleep in my room! Then if I get sick in the middle of the night, he'll be there to take care of me.'' He grinned across the table, as if there could be no fault found in that plan. "I sleep in the top bunk, but if you really want it, I'll let you sleep up there tonight. It's pretty high, though.''

"I'll keep that in mind,'' Gabe wondered when, exactly, that gap-toothed smile was going to lose its charm. So far, he was finding it nearly impossible to resist. "I've never slept in a bunk bed.''

"You wouldn't like it,'' Katherine informed him briskly. "Trust me.''

"He would too like it, wouldn't ya, Gabe?''

"He wouldn't like it,'' Katherine said through lips drawn tight with desperation, lips that Gabe couldn't decide if he found intriguing because he knew he'd once kissed them or because he wanted to kiss them again. "Your mother's probably right,'' he said. "I'm used to sleeping in a big bed.''

"That's okay,'' Abby said. "Mom has a big bed, don't ya, Mom?''

"Yeah,'' Andy agreed. "We can all sleep in it. That'd be cool!''

The fork, with half a french fry still attached,

clanked against the table. Katherine looked at Gabe, a plea for help in her stormy gray eyes and—he wanted to believe—a few lightning flashes of awareness, as well. He would have liked to say something to distract the twins from their energetic planning and maybe win a smile of gratitude from their mother. But he couldn't think of a single thing to say...not when he was so distracted by the thought of Katherine in Katherine's bed.

With a sigh, she jerked her gaze away from his. "Put on your coats," she said to the twins. "It's time we went home."

"Okay, Mom." Abby grabbed up her Toss-and-Comb Tresses Tina, the toy Gabe had bought for her in Macy's after the incident in Santa's House. Scrambling to her feet, she leaned over the divider into the next booth. "Gabe's goin' home with us tonight," she told the couple, clearly warming to any agenda that included Gabe. "He's gonna sleep with our mom."

"Abby!" Katherine, her cheeks tinged pink, all but jumped from the booth. "Into your coat," she said crisply, shaking out Abby's pink parka. "Now, please."

Gabe was on his feet an instant later, holding Andy's purple parka as if he and Katherine had rehearsed this same drill a dozen times. "Come on, buddy," he said. "Put your coat on."

Grabbing his Jet Jupiter rocket ship, Andy leaped to his feet and stomped his way across the bench seat, stopping only long enough to inform the neighbors, "I gotta go. They're in a *big* hurry to go to bed!"

Gabe captured Andy's arms with the coat sleeves and pulled him out of the booth before some other guileless indiscretion could get them booted out of the restaurant. By the time he had Andy in his parka, Abby was zipped, mittened and hooded, as well, and Katherine was struggling to hold on to her daughter while putting on her own long black wool coat. "Let me help," Gabe said, eager to have an excuse to brush his fingers across the back of her neck and touch the dark blond strands of hair that were about to be captured beneath her coat collar.

"Thank you," she said, thrusting Abby's mittened fingers into his outstretched hand. "Whatever you do, don't let go of her."

Abby's smile was innocently delighted. "Hey, Gabe, do we hafta go home now? It's barely even dark outside. Couldn't we have some more fun?"

"More fun?" he repeated, unable to put his finger on the *fun* they'd apparently already had. "I think that's a question you'll have to ask your mom."

"You ask her. If we ask her, she'll say no."

Andy tugged on Gabe's shirtsleeve. "Can you tie this for me?" He held on to two long cords that had been pulled until the hood of his jacket puckered around his face. "But don't tie it in a bow. Bows are for girls."

Gabe bent to tie the requested strings and to unobtrusively loosen the hood before it cut off all circulation to the kid's nose. "Men can be beaus," he said.

"I don't *think* so." Andy held his chin high for easy access. "Mom, guys can't be bows, can they?"

Katherine pulled on her gloves. "If it's spelled *b-o-w*, no, a guy can't be a bow. But it it's spelled *b-e-a-u*, then yes, a guy can."

"Well, I'm not a bow," Andy snapped his chin downward in affirmation. "And neither is Gabe."

"If Mom says he's a bow, he's a bow." Abby tried to tuck her Tresses Tina doll into her pocket. "Mom? Is Gabe a bow?"

"I don't know," Katherine said, her eyes meeting his hesitantly, but with definite curiosity. "Are you someone's beau?"

"Not at the moment." He straightened to offer her a slow, I'm-available kind of grin. "But I've recently met someone who could tie me in knots without half trying."

"Could her name be...Sheila?" Katherine asked sweetly, counteroffering what he considered to be an unreasonably self-righteous smile.

Abby tugged on his sleeve and gave him a blue-eyed gaze of the utmost gravity. "Gabe, Sheila was not a real elf. Her fingernails were *blue*."

Andy looked solemnly at his rocket ship. "If I have to be a bow, can I be a bow weevil? That's a beetle bug. And I'd rather be a beetle bug than a bow tie."

"It's not that kind of bow, Andy." Katherine bent to him, as if she were about to retie the knotted strings under his hood, but Gabe grabbed her gloved hand and drew it out of harm's way. "And it's a boll wee—"

"Let him be a bow weevil," Gabe requested softly. "Because, frankly, I think trying to explain the difference between bow, beau, and a beetle bug could get very embarrassing."

"I'll just explain about homonyms and—"

"They already think we're going to sleep together, Katherine. Let's not introduce a whole new concept in male-female relationships just now."

She looked straight at him, and he felt the impact of attraction all the way to his toes. "We are not going to sleep together," she said, going straight to the heart of the matter...and revealing that her thoughts had been running along the same tracks as his.

"No, we're not," he agreed easily. "Not tonight, anyway." He turned quickly to the kids, before she could make some other denial she'd only have to retract later. "Now, kiddos, what did you say you wanted to do? See the Christmas tree at Rockefeller Center?"

"Yeah!" Abby jumped up and down and clapped her mittened hands. "The Christmas tree! The Christmas tree!"

Andy joined her in joyous bouncing. "The Christmas tree! We get to see the Christmas tree!"

Devious, but deadly, Gabe thought, as he anticipated Katherine's frown and lifted his shoulder in a I'm-not-telling-them-they-can't-see-the-tree, *you*-tell-them kind of shrug. Until she walked into his office yesterday, he hadn't realized what a devious person he could be. But he was learning. Until yesterday, he'd actually believed children should be seen and not heard, but after the past few hours, he was all for letting them do his talking for him. So far, their ideas had been a damn sight better than his.

ABBY TIPPED HER HEAD BACK as far as it would go and looked straight up. "That's the biggest, *best* Christmas tree in the whole world."

"I could climb that sucker in two seconds," Andy decreed.

Katherine put her hand on the nylon hood to keep him from following through on *that* idea, and discovered Gabe's hand there before her. He had on gloves and so did she, but still, the warmth, the unexpectedness, of the contact made her catch her breath, and she would have drawn back if he hadn't done so first, leaving her in charge of her son...if not her pulse rate. "This is a tree, not a sucker, which is not a good word to use in this instance." She kept her hand on his head, maintaining a firm control of his impulsive nature, and though her voice had half a mind to be breathless, she brought it under control, too. "And this tree is for looking at, not climbing."

"But, Mom, I'm never gonna get to climb a tree!"

"Never's a long time."

"But if nobody climbs it, how do they get all those decorations on there?" Abby turned her wind-rosy face in a perfect three-point rotation to look from Katherine to Gabe to the tree. "That's what I want to know."

"We could ask one of the policemen." Katherine indicated one of the many officers assigned to the area at this time of year. She liked to give the twins every opportunity to interact with policemen so that they'd learn respect and a degree of trust for the men and women who enforced the laws. "Maybe they could tell you how it's done, Abby."

"Don't ask a policeman," Gabe said. "They're just going to tell you a bunch of city employees decorated the tree using a bucket truck and long poles with hooks on the end of them."

Katherine tried to look pleasant as she frowned at him. "Is there something *wrong* with that explanation?"

"Not if you just want the facts, ma'am."

Sooner or later, Katherine was going to wipe that smile off his face. She just hadn't decided when or how, yet. "I think children need facts. I think they need to know they're getting truthful answers to their questions."

The corners of his mouth quirked upward as he looked at the huge Christmas tree. "An explanation doesn't have to be stripped bare of magic to be truthful, you know."

He must believe she had no imagination whatsoever, Katherine thought. Her glance fell to the careless drift of his topcoat and the roguish drape of the black plaid scarf around his neck and the set of his shoulders and the angle of his jaw, and the fine lines around his eyes, his mouth.... Boy, was he wrong. "All right, Gabe, let's hear your explanation as to how the decorations got on this tree."

He glanced down at the eager expressions on the twins' faces and cleared his throat. "It's only a theory."

"Something like your the-*real*-Santa-can-be-found-at-Macy's theory?"

When his gaze moved to her, Katherine felt a shiver that had nothing to do with the crisp December weather and everything to do with the warm censure in his brown eyes. "You, Kate, are a skeptic."

"I didn't think you'd noticed."

"What's that?" Abby asked.

"Yeah, what's a sh-sheptick?" Andy floundered over the unfamiliar syllables. "What'd ya call her?"

"A skeptic," Gabe supplied readily. "That's a person who doesn't believe in Santa Claus."

"Ohhhhhh..." The twins favored Katherine with identical nods of superior understanding. "She doesn't believe there's such a thing as elves, either," Abby said on a sad sigh.

"Yeah," Andy agreed, although he didn't sigh. "She wouldn't believe you, no matter if you told her *everything* about Santa and the elves. She wouldn't believe you even if you told her what makes the reindeer fly. She wouldn't believe you if you told her—"

She interrupted the litany of her disbeliefs with a soft tap on the purple parka's hood. "He got the point, Andy."

"I got the point," Gabe said, meeting her eyes. "I just don't want to believe it."

Katherine swallowed hard, knowing he probably thought she had stamped out every spark of fantasy in her own life and wouldn't be satisfied until she'd stamped them out of Abby's and Andy's lives, as well. But that wasn't it, at all. She simply didn't want them to be hurt, as she had been, by believing in something that could never be true. With a lift of her chin, she silently challenged him to prove her wrong. "I suppose you have a theory on flying reindeer, too."

"They eat special hay," Andy informed her. "It grows and the apes pick it and carry it to the North Pole, but Rudolph eats more than anybody else and that's why his nose is red!"

Gabe took a moment to digest that before he looked at Katherine with a noncommittal frown. "Except for the part about the red nose and the apes, that's pretty much the gist of the theory."

Abby pulled on his coat, again, with more than a little impatience. "Are you ever gonna tell me how that all those balls got on the tree?"

"Yes." Gabe patted her mittened hand and squinted at the Christmas tree. "I'm going to tell you right now...just as soon as I remember."

"How could you forget, when you have such an *excellent* memory?" The words were out of Katherine's mouth before she stopped to think...and there was no mistaking her sanctimonious tone, either.

He smiled, the forgetful son-of-a-gun. "I only want to be sure I remember *all* the details."

Abby's sigh was long-suffering. "Would you please start 'membering, now?"

"Okay," he said. "My dad told me this story when I was just about your age, and it starts like this... A long time ago, at least a hundred years, a little boy...and his sister...found a pinecone they believed was magic. They planted it at the edge of a—"

"How come?" Andy asked.

Gabe frowned. "Because they wanted it to grow."

"No, how come they knew it was magic?"

"Well...I don't know," Gabe admitted. "What would make you think something was magic?"

"I had a magic wand once," Abby said. "It sparkled."

"That's because it had glitter inside it," Andy told her with a brotherly degree of intolerance. "But it wasn't magic. It was just a dumb stick."

"It was not."

"Was too. Only a *girl* would think it was magic."

Abby gave her head a toss. "Well, I think the pinecone sparkled like a star and that's how come they knew it was magic."

"That's dumb," Andy stated flatly. "I think a big, scary monster jumped out from behind a tree and told them it was magic. Did a monster tell 'em it was magic, Gabe? Was it a green or purple monster?"

Gabe looked momentarily at a loss, but he recovered at least some of his equilibrium. "It might have been a monster with red and green fish scales on it. Or the pinecone could have been a sparkling star that fell out of the sky. Or it could have been that the children were very smart and just knew. But however they found out it was magic, they planted it and watered it and waited for it to grow."

"Like Jack and the beanstalk?" Abby pressed her hands tightly together, as she stared, enthralled, at the storyteller. "Was it magic like that?"

"Something like that, yes. The tree grew up full of the dreams the children had whispered into it as a seedling, and it dreamed of being in a special place where lots and lots of children could see how beautifully it was decorated. So one night, while the whole world was asleep, the tree wished a big wish, and the next morning it was here, in Rockefeller Center, and it was covered in sparkling lights and shiny monster-sized ornaments and everyone who saw it thought it was magic.''

He smiled broadly at Katherine, obviously pleased, obviously believing he'd pulled off a coup the size of Manhattan, obviously unaware that he'd left out a few *details*.

''But how did it get here?'' Abby asked on a practical note. ''Trees can't walk.''

''The monster carried it, didn't he, Gabe?''

Abby stamped her foot. ''There wasn't a stupid monster, Andy. Only a *boy* would think there was.''

Andy made a face at her. She wrinkled her nose at him. Katherine gave a tug to each neon-colored hood, and Andy returned to the attack on Gabe's imaginative theory. ''Did it fly through space? On a rocket ship?'' Jet Jupiter's ship was brought out of the pocket to illustrate how this could have been accomplished. ''See? It could've fit right in there and been here in a nanosecond.''

''But the decorations would have gotten broken that way.'' Abby, clearly, wasn't impressed with space travel. ''And the lights have to be plugged in somewhere. How did the lights get all the way up at the top, Gabe? Did they grow on the tree, too?''

''Lights can't grow on trees.'' Andy whizzed the rocket ship past her ear. ''And the decorations wouldn't get broken. They'd burn up, instead, 'cause it's really hot in outer space.''

"Is not," Abby said.

"Is too," Andy argued.

Katherine smiled, enjoying one of the rare moments when she was completely thrilled by her children's insatiable and stubborn curiosity and their random leaps of logic. "You could still ask the policeman," she suggested in an offhand manner, as if she didn't care one way or the other. "There's one standing right over there."

Andy made a split-second decision. "Yeah, let's ask him if he saw the rocket ship." He turned on a dime and, with Abby only a few steps behind, he raced the ten feet or so to where the policeman stood.

Leaving Gabe at Katherine's mercy.

"I'm afraid they didn't believe your theory." She tried not to sound smug. She really did. But a tiny conceit crept into her voice...totally without her permission. Well, maybe not totally. "Magic is a difficult concept at their age."

He shifted his weight and looked, again, at the wonderful tree. "Believing in magic is normal at seven, Kate. It's only after that it becomes a difficult concept."

She followed his gaze to the biggest, *best* tree in the whole world and remembered a time when she had been seven and believed.

For the space of a heartbeat, or possibly two, she wished she could tell Gabe about that magic moment in her life, but "Don't call me Kate" was all she was able to say.

Chapter Six

"This was a good idea, wasn't it, Mom?" Abby held Katherine's hand happily as they waited in a line that stretched from the sidewalk in front of Saks's windows on Fifth Avenue all the way around the corner onto Forty-ninth Street. "I'm *sooooo* glad that policeman thought of it. Aren't you, Mom? Me and Andy might have never thought about seeing the windows if that policeman hadn't asked us if we'd already seen it. We coulda missed this!"

"We could have," Katherine dutifully replied, turning her collar up against the chill and wishing she could get her hands on that policeman, right now. "And it would be terrible to miss seeing the Saks Christmas display tonight, even though we *could* always come back another day when there isn't such a long line."

"But we like waitin' in line, don't we, Mom?" Abby smiled, her teeth flashing white against the bright color the cold had lent her cheeks. "Do ya think it'll be much longer, Mom? How long have we been standin' here? Ten minutes? What time is it? This line's movin' faster than Macy's line did, isn't it? A *lot* faster. Don't you think this is fun, Mom? I think this is really fun. Hey, Andy, look! It's Isabelle!''

Andy stopped battering Gabe with a similar barrage of chatter to wave frantically at a little girl with blond curls just peeking out from the hood of her navy blue coat. "Hey! Issy! Over here!''

The girl looked, smiled, and pulled on the hands she was holding...obviously the hands of her parents, as she looked remarkably like both of them. As the traffic light changed and the threesome approached, Katherine prayed that this was another Isabelle, and not the Isabelle of the Saint Julian's playground disaster. But she had a feeling her children wouldn't have been quite so glad to see any other Isabelle. Abby and Andy would fight the world to protect each other, but they shared an eager admiration for anyone who dared stand against them.

Katherine looked closely at the man and woman and hoped they wouldn't make the connection between these redheaded, freckle-faced twins and the redheaded, freckle-faced twins who'd dogpiled their daughter. On the plus side, Issy appeared perfectly happy to meet up with the dynamic duo. On the minus side, Andy was asking to see the scrape on Issy's elbow, the one she'd received when she fell...after he pushed her.

Of all times for her son to be articulate, Katherine thought, and smiled awkwardly at the adults. "You must be Isabelle's parents," she said. "I'm Katherine Harmon.''

"Ron and Reba Kinser." Isabelle's father didn't

smile, but he did extend his hand to Gabe. "Mr. Harmon."

"Housley," Gabe corrected along with the handshake. "Gaberson Housley."

The Kinsers traded a knowing glance that, for some reason, set Katherine's teeth on edge. "Nice to meet you," one or both of the Kinsers murmured. "We're on our way to see the Christmas tree," Reba Kinser offered by way of being polite.

"We just came from there," Katherine answered, thinking they just might slide through this without unpleasantness.

"Isabelle brought her ice skates." Reba indicated the bag she carried. "She was practically skating before she walked, you know, and performs regularly with the Junior Olympians. But at Christmas, she loves to take a couple of turns on the ice at Rockefeller Center. It's one of our special Christmas traditions." She smiled adoringly at the top of Issy's hooded head. "You should bring your children over to watch. Her instructor says Isabelle is the most talented student he's ever had the pleasure of working with, and everyone agrees she's simply incredible when she skates."

And when she doesn't, Katherine thought, feeling the tug of one-upmanship, knowing it would be petty—and impertinent—to point out that her twins had bested the incredible Isabelle in a playground battle of wits. "Oh, I wish we could," she said instead. "But I don't think Abby and Andy would be able to sit still long enough to really appreciate Isabelle's talent."

Reba looked down at the children...at the exact moment Andy demonstrated the incredible talent of crossing his eyes while sticking his thumbs in his ears and a finger up each nostril. When Reba raised her head, there was a hint of compassion in her smile. "No, I suppose not."

"Maybe there'll be another opportunity to watch Isabelle skate," she said, because it would have been childish and rude to kick Reba in the shins. Katherine was beginning to understand how the playground incident had come about.

"Skate?" Abby, who could pick out a topic of interest to her from amid a dozen conversations, looked hopefully at Katherine. "We didn't get to ice-skate."

"No, you didn't."

"We still could," Abby suggested.

"No, we couldn't."

"Yes, we could, Mom."

"Not tonight." Katherine gave Abby the stern don't-argue-with-me frown before turning to the Kinsers with the standard maternal Mona Lisa smile...a curve of the lips, a soft look in the eyes, pride in every nuance of expression, as if she couldn't imagine ever losing patience with these fruits of her loins. "Such energy," she said. "They want to do everything at once, all in the same day. Frankly, I'm exhausted and feel like we've been downtown for days, instead of only hours."

"We spent all afternoon at Macy's." Gabe left his stilted conversation with Ron to lend Katherine some support. "Waiting to see Santa."

Ron Kinser managed to look even more disapproving than he had before. "You took them out of school to go to Macy's?"

"They're out of school for the holidays," Gabe said, a defensive note threading its way into his tone.

"They were suspended, Daddy." Isabelle already had her permanent front teeth, and she pronounced every word distinctly. "Remember, Daddy, these are the first-graders I told you about."

"We did not get ssssustended!" Andy, who had proudly told everyone from the doorman to the waitress that he and his sister had gotten kicked out of school, took umbrage when Issy stated it. "We got extra vacation 'cause Sister Mary Cornelia wanted us to."

Isabelle nodded. So did Reba. So did Ron. Katherine had never seen three such condescending nods. "Oops, the line's moving," she said. "We'd better not hold things up." But when she and Gabe propelled the twins forward into the next roped-off queue, Isabelle's chiding singsong syllables came with them. "You got suspended."

"We did not!" Abby whirled, ducking under Katherine's protective hand to face off with her tormentor. "Sister Mary Cornelia wanted us to have extra time to have fun with our mom and our dad."

Katherine gulped, but Andy plowed into that idea before she could stop him. "Yeah! And that's what we been doin'! Havin' fun with our mom and dad."

"You don't have a dad." Isabelle wasn't backing down, either, and her silly parents obviously thought she knew what she was talking about. Which, unfor-

tunately, she did. "You told the whole school that
your mother had to go to the sperm bank to get you,
remember?"

There was not exactly a collective gasp from the
crowd, but heads turned, and in a sort of unanimous
gaze, all eyes were on Katherine, who couldn't help
but think there had to be easier ways to die of embarrassment.

"Well...yeah, so what?" Abby raised her pointy
little chin. "She had to meet Gabe there so he could
give her the sperm and be our dad!"

Wanting nothing more than to fall through a crack
in the sidewalk, Katherine gathered two handfuls of
neon-colored parkas and spun the twins around and
in front of her in the line. But Abby wasn't through
setting Isabelle straight, and she wiggled around
Katherine and exercised her vocal cords. "And our
dad knows everything there is to know about Santa
Claus. He knows where he lives and the names of
all the elves, too!"

Andy, too, ignored Katherine's furious and hissing
Sssshhhhh! "Yeah, and he knows how come Rudolph has a red nose instead of a black one like all
the other reindeer and he knows where the apes get
the hay and he bought me this cool rocket ship!"
The toy was thrust into the air with all the attitude a
seven-year-old boy could muster...and promptly
commandeered by his red-faced mother.

"Andrew. Abigail. Don't say another word."
Katherine squeezed their shoulders to be certain they
knew how serious she was...as if they could ignore
the absolute authority in her voice. She wouldn't al-

low herself to feel the curious stares of everyone within earshot of her children, didn't dare look at Gabe, couldn't bear to imagine what he was thinking, didn't even want to consider his appalled silence. If they hadn't been caught within the parameters of the roped-off sidewalk and a good-size crowd, she would have run, screaming, down the street, dragging the twins every step. And she wouldn't have stopped until she reached Nebraska. Or Iowa. Whichever was farther.

Then she felt a reassuring arm around her waist, was pulled comfortingly against a strong, supportive—and very male—body, and heard Gabe's soothing "It could have been worse, you know. Imagine how you'd feel if they'd claimed Howard Stern was their father."

Katherine felt the hot push of tears behind her eyes and wondered how it would feel to bury her face in his shoulder and, for just a minute, turn her back on the responsibilities and choices of her lifetime. But when the minute was over, she'd still be embarrassed and she'd have gotten mascara on his Armani coat. She risked a glance, promptly got lost in his tenderness, and forgot that her favorite thing about him was that damn coat. "I'm sorry they dragged you into this."

"Hey, don't apologize. I'm flattered as hell."

She rolled her eyes. "Oh, right. Sure you are."

His smile felt better to her than a Looney Tunes Band-Aid on a paper cut. "I am," he said with a good show of sincerity. "They're great kids, Katherine. A little too uninhibited, maybe. A little too mouthy, for sure. But great kids. You've done a wonderful job with them, no matter who else contributed to their DNA.''

"Mom?'' Andy wiggled under the grip she still had on his shoulder. "Can I have my rocket ship back, now?''

Abby, who had never stopped wiggling, just changed directions and began to hop up and down. "And can I have my Toss-and-Comb Tresses Tina?''

Katherine didn't want to move away from Gabe's warm comfort, but she knew better than to linger too long. He was, after all, a man. And he wasn't, after all, a part of her real life. Straightening, she plunged her hands into her pockets and pulled out Andy's rocket ship and a glove full of...nothing. Handing the one toy to Andy, she looked questioningly at Abby's expectant face. "I don't have your doll, Abby. Didn't you put her in your pocket?''

Abby patted her coat from hem to hood, and her blue eyes rounded in alarm. "She's gone! *Oh, no!* Toss-and-Comb Tresses Tina is missing!''

THE WATER pouring from the tap into the bathtub was lukewarm...at best. The bottle of Harner's Luxurious Rose-Petal Bath Foam contained some strange substance that didn't bubble and smelled like suntan lotion. A relaxing soak in the tub had sounded like the perfect end to a very long day, but, as with the day itself, nothing had gone as Katherine planned.

"Mom! Tell Abby to stop windin' up her music box! I can't go to sleep when it keeps playin' that stupid song!''

"It is not a stupid song! You're just a stupid brother! Mom! Tell Andy to stop botherin' me so I can go to sleep!"

With a sigh, Katherine turned the tap as high as it would go and flipped open the tub's drain to release the accumulation of water. She wasn't going to get the bath, obviously, but at least the sound of running water would help insulate her until her two overly tired children finally fell asleep. She'd ordered them not to get out of bed for any reason, but they'd figure out an emergency in seconds if they discovered she wasn't actually in the bath. And she was in no mood to monitor their last stand against the sandman.

Using extreme caution, she turned the knob, eased the door open and slipped quietly into the hall, carefully and almost silently, pulling the door closed behind her. She moved down the hallway like a stealth bomber, feeling her way past the kitchen door and tiptoeing across the front room carpet to the bay window.

Her view of Central Park was bathed in the soft night darkness and shadowed in pools of streetlights. Snow was starting to fall, a snowflake here and there, an inch due by morning. The weatherman had predicted a perfect New York day for tomorrow, though. Clear skies, no precipitation, and just cold enough to add interest to the cheeks. Or so he'd said.

Not that she needed any more *interest* in her cheeks. They still felt flushed from the accumulated blushes of the day. Just thinking about the abrupt goodbye Gabe had said at their door only an hour ago brought the heat rushing back with a vengeance.

Not that she'd expected him to want to stick around, but she could now admit to feeling just a tad disappointed that he'd been in such a hurry to get away. She didn't blame him, of course. If their circumstances had been reversed, she would have said goodbye and good riddance in the lobby.

The twins had whined, fussed and demanded attention. They'd begged, screamed, cried and thrown up. They'd eaten everything in sight, asked for more, and spent Gabe's money as if it were hers. They'd manipulated, wheedled and gotten their way. And then they'd had to make matters worse by declaring him their long-lost genetic link. If she'd been in his shoes, she'd have been halfway to Tibet by now, just to be certain that kind of announcement didn't happen again.

It wouldn't. She'd already had a talk with Abby and Andy about their behavior and made some strong suggestions for improvement. Or else. They hadn't asked the obvious: *Or else what?* Which was a good thing, considering she had yet to figure that part out, herself.

The phone rang, startling her with its suddenness, its urgency, and she reached for it blindly, grasping it just before the ringer could go off again. "Hello?"

"Don't hang up!" It was Gabe's voice. His firm, desperate voice. "Please!"

"Okay," she said quietly, and then, just to make certain he wouldn't think she recognized his voice, she asked, "Who is this?"

"Katherine! Don't hang up!"

Her lips curved at the sound of his evident relief. "Are you sure you have the right number?"

"Don't hang up, Katherine. This is Gabe Housley. I've been calling for the past twenty minutes...and getting a gruff, muffled voice telling me either it's past my bedtime, or I'm going to get in trouble for making obscene phone calls, or that my refrigerator is running and I'd better go catch it. Then the line goes dead."

"Hmm. Sounds serious. Maybe you should report this to the phone company."

"I'm reporting it to the mother."

"Which makes you a tattletale. How do you know you didn't dial someone else's number and talk to their children?"

"I recognized the giggles. Are they finally asleep?"

"I don't know. Why don't you ask them? Andy? Abby? Are you out of bed again?"

There was a dual gasp, and then a click and a clearer line as the extension phone was cradled. Far down the hall, Katherine heard the patter of running feet, some hushed conversation, and then the double thump as they each hit their respective mattresses. "They're not asleep yet," she told Gabe. "And on top of that, you've just blown my cover. Until I answered the phone, they thought I was taking a bath. Now I'll probably have to tuck them into bed all over again."

"I thought they'd be so tired, you'd have trouble keeping them awake long enough to get them in their pajamas and brush their teeth."

"I wish. They're so keyed up, I'm not sure they're ever going to settle down."

"In that case, I'm sorry I left in such a hurry. I figured it would make your life easier if I wasn't around."

As if a man had ever made her life easier, Katherine thought as she turned back to the window. "Well, they're in bed now, and as long as the phone doesn't ring again, maybe they'll go to sleep."

"Then the obvious solution is to keep talking to me so the line stays busy and the phone can't ring."

"I was actually thinking about going to bed myself."

The instant and ensuing pause fairly crackled with possibilities and, when Gabe cleared his throat, a tremor of awareness raced down Katherine's spine.

"I enjoyed today," he said.

She found herself smiling. "You sound surprised."

He gave a short laugh. "I am. I never thought I liked kids before, but Andy and Abby are, uh, interesting."

At least he hadn't said cute. "Yes, sometimes they're so *interesting*, I can hardly stand it."

There was another pause, this one reflective. "On a scale of zero to ten, how *interesting* a day was it?"

"Well, if zero is when they're asleep and ten is one hell of a day, I'd say we reached a high seven."

He seemed to consider that with some trepidation. "I guess that means tomorrow they might say something really interesting."

This time she laughed. "Not if I can help it, they

won't. I'm keeping them off street corners for at least a week.''

He laughed with her, and Katherine thought how nice it felt to share a lighthearted amusement over some of the not-so-splendid moments of parenthood.

''I really enjoyed today,'' he said again.

''You already said that.''

''I was hoping you might respond by saying you enjoyed today, too.''

Katherine pursed her lips, wondering where this was going and how she wanted to handle it. ''Today was...not what I expected. The twins enjoyed themselves excessively and I enjoyed being with them, even though their behavior left a lot to be desired.''

''I thought they behaved very well.''

''Easy for you to say.''

''You have to admit the circumstances were less than ideal.''

She had to laugh. ''That would be about the nicest thing anyone could say, considering that the day's high point was finding Tresses Tina still at the diner and the low was—'' Katherine stopped in midsentence. The low point, of course, was the humiliating moments in front of Saks...moments Gabe had to be nearly as embarrassed about as she was herself. ''I don't usually say, 'I told you so,' but...''

''I take full responsibility for the original idea, but the circumstances were clearly not my fault.''

''Mmm-hmm. It's clearly *not* your fault that Andy drank three cups of hot chocolate and ate God knows how many jelly beans.''

''I had to give him whatever he wanted. Otherwise, he'd have told you I coached him on what to say to get us out of line."

"You did that?"

"You mean he hasn't already confessed? Damn. I should have kept my mouth shut. Obviously I underestimated the kid."

Katherine shook her head at her own indefinable reflection in the window. "No, you didn't. He'll tell me all about your devious behavior the minute he remembers. Andy's better than Abby at keeping secrets, but that's not saying a lot."

"Does that mean they've already spilled the beans about tomorrow?"

"Tomorrow?" she repeated, feeling an odd mixture of anticipation and dread. "Please tell me you didn't make plans with them for tomorrow. No, on second thought, don't tell me. Because even if you did, your plans just got canceled."

"You can join us."

"Thank you, but I've already planned to take the twins to the Plaza for lunch, and then to a museum. They need some educational field trips to balance out all the excesses of the Christmas holiday. Providing they're not both sick tonight, which wouldn't surprise me, after all the junk they ate today."

"I was supposed to spend the night to cover just such a potentiality, wasn't I? Say the word and I'll be there in fifteen minutes. Or less."

The last two words were softer—intimate, somehow—and the tremor took another dive down her back. "The word is no. Definitely no."

"You're absolutely certain?"

"No!" The thought of him here, with her, after the twins were finally asleep, the two of them watching the snow fall. Or finding something better to do. The tremor settled into an indeterminate ache inside her.

"So you're not certain I shouldn't come over?"

"No," she repeated. "Yes. *Don't* come over."

"Well, okay," he said on a sigh. "But I was really hoping I'd get a shot at that upper bunk."

As if Andy would really let anyone else sleep there. Andy? she thought. Who was she kidding? As if *she* would let Gabe sleep anywhere but with her. If he was here. Which, fortunately, he wasn't. Katherine squared her shoulders, shoving fantasy rudely out of her way. "After today's fiasco, Gabe, I can't believe you're eager to spend the night in a bunk bed. In fact, after today, I figured you'd be very busy, keeping up with the elves and their pertinent data and all. I didn't think we'd see much of you, and I certainly didn't expect to get a good-night call tonight."

She expected him to laugh with relieved agreement, make a halfhearted denial, then bring the conversation to a polite close, glad to be free of her and her mouthy children. But he didn't laugh. He didn't make any denial, halfhearted or otherwise. He didn't say anything at all for a very long moment.

"I had a specific reason for calling, Katherine," he said, a clear reluctance in each word. "I thought about this all the way home and, well, I have to ask you something. For my own peace of mind. After what was said today, I think I have a right to...well, maybe not a right... Ah, hell, there isn't a good way to phrase this, so I'm just going to blurt it out and hope you won't hang up on me.''

Katherine closed her eyes, praying he wouldn't ask, knowing he was going to, wishing there was some answer that wouldn't be bluntly honest. "Yes," she said, unable to keep from plunging into the embarrassing subject before he made it worse by asking. "I used a sperm bank, and no, there's no possibility you were the donor.''

There was a pause, marked by a sharp inhale on his end of the line. "Well, hell, of course there isn't! I've never... That was *not* what I was going to ask you. I only wanted to know about the kiss...whether I called you someone else's name or said anything that would help me remember.... Jeez. And I thought *that* was going to be an embarrassing question.'' He sounded distressed, and she could imagine him impatiently brushing that recalcitrant lock of hair off his forehead. "It never would have occurred to me you'd think that *I* might think I could be the father of your twins." He stopped and took another deep, audible breath. "For your information, Katherine, that is not my idea of a charitable donation."

And she had thought the day couldn't get any more embarrassing. "Sorry. It just seemed like the obvious question.''

"It isn't obvious. It isn't any of my business. It isn't anyone's business, and you've been dating the wrong men if that's the kind of thing they ask you about.''

There was nothing for it now but to buck up and explain as best she could. "Believe it or not, conception isn't high on my list of preferred topics to discuss over dinner. And the subject has never been open for casual conversation...at least, it wasn't until a couple of months ago, when the twins shared the miraculous story of their 'virgin birth' with the students and faculty at Saint Julian's. They had a, uh, little trouble differentiating between in vitro and the Immaculate Conception.''

His hesitation was brief, but ponderous. "And I was worried about confusing them with *bow* and *beau.*"

"When they asked the question, I felt they deserved a truthful answer."

"For Pete's sake, what question did they ask?"

"The where-did-I-come-from question. Most children ask that when they're four or five."

"I guess New York City isn't good enough?"

"They get more information than that from Saturday morning cartoons."

"So you told them everything you knew about the birds, the bees and the, uh, bank."

She bristled a bit. "I didn't use the term *sperm bank* if that's what you're getting at. I don't know where they picked that up, unless someone at the fertility clinic used it."

"You took them to a fertility clinic?"

"Not *a* clinic. *The* clinic."

"Of course, *the* clinic," he said, surprise and a subtle exasperation blending into his tone. "I wouldn't have expected you to take them on a tour of just any clinic. That would be like telling a lie."

She pulled the phone from her ear for a second

and frowned irritably at it. "I suppose you would have told them they were delivered by the stork."

"No, I would have saved at least half the truth about reproductive science until they had a grasp of basic biology."

"They didn't seem to have too much trouble grasping the concept of reproduction."

"It's the concept of privacy—*your* privacy—they don't seem to understand."

She opened her mouth to argue further, but closed it with a sigh. "Believe me, if I'd known they were going to repeat everything, no matter how inappropriate, I'd never have taught them to talk."

"In your defense, Kate, there isn't anything wrong with the truth. It's just that it so often *sounds* inappropriate."

"I should have waited until they were older...at least until they could make some distinction between a private matter and keeping a secret. But I was determined not to hide the truth of their conception. I didn't want them to think there could ever be anything wrong or shameful about not having a father."

"A dad," he corrected softly.

"A dad," she repeated, feeling the uncertainty of her decision arise all over again. A father could be anybody, but a dad was a presence. And a dad was what she had decided her children would be okay without. Now, for better or worse, she had to stand by that decision. "Look, Gabe, this is probably as good a time as any to ask you to call off this so-called Santa search. It was one thing for you to play along when the twins came to your office, wanting to hire a detective. But it's something entirely different when you spend the day with them and they start to imagine you could be their father. They don't believe in Santa Claus. They're not going to believe in Santa Claus. And…I don't want them to start believing in you."

There was a startled silence from his end of the line, then, "Kate, I—"

"Don't call me that, please." She hadn't planned on doing this over the phone, but she was basically a coward and she wasn't sure she had the courage to say it to his face. "It was nice of you to take an interest in Abby and Andy. I appreciate your good intentions, even though I wish you hadn't acted on them. I know you've told the kids you'll keep looking for the *real* Santa Claus until you find him, but they think they're joining you in the search. I've already explained to them that isn't going to happen, and now I'm telling you. There is no Santa Claus, Gabe. No Kris Kringle. No Father Christmas. No jolly old Saint Nicholas, who's going to leave a gift-wrapped *dad* under their Christmas tree. Please don't complicate their lives."

"*Their* lives, Katherine? Or yours?"

Gathering her waning courage, she took a deep breath. "I'm asking you to leave us alone."

"Somehow, that didn't sound much like a request."

She swallowed the sudden dryness in her throat. "An astute observation."

This time, his pause was marked by a strained silence. "You're going to be disappointed if you expect me to say an obedient goodbye and hang up."

"Then let me do it for you."

"Don't hang up, Katherine, unless you want to find me at your door in about fifteen minutes, because this discussion isn't over. Not by a long shot."

"There is nothing to discuss." She fought to keep any trace of panic out of her voice. "They're my children."

"And my clients."

"Oh, please, don't bring up that ridiculous contract, Gabe. It isn't even a written agreement, just a pretense to persuade two innocent children you're not a real con artist."

"It may be a pretense to you, Kate, but it isn't to Abby and Andy. And it isn't to me, either. It's as close to a commitment to anyone or anything as I've come since my divorce five years ago, and I'm not going to back away from it because you think it's silly."

"Silly and dangerous."

"To who? The twins? Or your perception that you can shelter them from the world and all its myriad lies? This isn't about Abby and Andy, Kate. It's about you. They didn't ask me to prove there's a Santa Claus for their benefit. They want you to believe, because if you don't, then neither can they."

"They're seven years old. A little young to have that much depth, don't you think?"

"Excuse me, but aren't you the mother who started them out reading Darwin's *The Origin of Species?*"

"That was uncalled-for."

"Yes, it was," he agreed, in an unexpected capitulation. "I apologize. But this is important to me. And it's important to them."

"I really don't care to discuss this with you," she said over a knot of anxiety so big the words came out with difficulty. "It isn't easy to raise two emotionally healthy children, but I'm doing my best. And, Gabe, I don't need or want any help."

"Your kids came to me, Katherine. I didn't draw their names out of a hat. They wanted a detective to find Santa Claus, who happens to be a missing person in their lives. Whether or not he exists in a physical form is beside the point. They're searching for Christmas, for a little magic to carry with them throughout their lives. Don't deny them that just because you're denying it to yourself."

Her hands began to shake, and she held the phone so tightly, her knuckles ached with the tension. "Goodbye, Gabe. Please don't call again."

"Kate, listen—"

She closed the door on a fantasy she had entertained for nearly a year, and slammed down the receiver before she could change her mind. There. It was done. Finished, before it had begun. Over, before he could get entangled in her life. Ended…before he could break all three of her hearts.

"Mommy?"

Katherine turned toward the sound and her daughter, who was standing just this side of the hallway with Matilda clutched tightly against her. Even in the dim light, Katherine could see the ominous flush on her cheeks. "What's wrong, Abby?" she asked.

"I don't feel too good." It was half whine, half entreaty and Katherine moved quickly toward the outstretched hands. Lifting Abby into her arms, Katherine headed for the bathroom, the bottle of Pepto-Bismol, and what promised to be a very long night.

Chapter Seven

Gabe dropped the phone into its cradle and stared morosely into the dark. "I am a jackass," he said.

"How can you tell, when you keep it as black as ink in here?" Gun entered the front room of the house they shared, tossing the impatient question ahead of him and switching on a flood of lights in his wake.

Blinking against the sudden brilliance, Gabe watched his father rumble around the room, dimming, adjusting and fiddling with the wattage until the place was lit up like a Christmas tree. The thought reminded him of being at Rockefeller Center, of watching Abby and Andy stare wide-eyed at the tree there, of watching Kate stare, too, of noticing the wistful, lonely look on her face. He slumped against the chair cushion and eyed his dad, who was settling into the leather recliner. "I thought you were on a stakeout."

Gun pushed back in the chair, bringing up the footrest. "Finished up the Casciano case this afternoon. Turned out to be insurance fraud, just like I said it would. Damn fine detective work on my part, if I do say so myself. Wouldn't be surprised if Mc-Clellan gave me a commendation for it.''

"Until you pay those damn fees to get a legitimate P.I. license, the only thing McClellan's likely to recommend you for is some hefty fines. He's the police chief, Dad. He can't be happy to have you skulking around out there playing 'gotcha' with his police force.''

"If he isn't, he ought to be.'' Folding his hands across his chest, Gun closed his eyes. "This city is one up on the bad guys tonight because I got out of bed this morning. Now, what the hell is wrong with you?''

"Other than knowing the police chief is about to issue a warrant for my father's arrest, what could possibly be wrong?''

Gun opened his eyes and narrowed them on Gabe. "You are worked up, aren't you?''

"It's been a long day.''

"Couldn't keep up with those kids, could you?''

Gabe's head came up with a snap. "How'd you know about that?''

"Which? The energy level of seven-year-olds or your lack of stamina?''

"Louisa could have told you I wasn't in the office, but I specifically did not tell her where I was or what I was doing, so how did you find out?''

"Simple deduction, Junior. You asked me where I'd go to look for Santa Claus, and I said Macy's.''

"I didn't say I was definitely going to take them.''

"Why would you go by yourself? The line is always long this close to Christmas, and you've never been the most patient person.''

Gabe stood and paced to the window, where he pulled back the drape. "It's snowing," he said, although about all he could see was the reflection of the thousand watts of light behind him. "We waited all afternoon, and when we finally got to the end of the line, the girl screamed like a banshee and the boy threw up at Santa's feet.''

Gun laughed. "I'll bet you took off like a rocket.''

"No, I took them to the Sixth Avenue Diner for a burger and fries." Gabe let the drape fall back into place. "Andy said he was hungry."

"You used to eat like a horse after you were sick to your stomach."

"I've never seen anything like them, Dad. They're constantly in motion, and they never stop talking. They're whiny and fretful and funny, and they say the most amazing things."

"Interesting."

"Yes," Gabe agreed, surprised that Gun understood. "I had no idea kids would be interesting. Katherine said..." His voice trailed off as he remembered the most recent things Katherine had said to him.

"Who's Katherine?"

"Their mother."

"Ah." Gun nodded, a glint of comprehension in his eyes. "Katherine. She's the one who doesn't think much of you."

Gabe dropped into the chair again, resuming his slouch. "She's the one."

"From the sound of it, today didn't do much to change her mind, either. In fact, it sort of sounded to me like she hung up on you."

"Is there some part of my private conversation you didn't overhear? Because I can fill in the details, if you missed any."

"No need to go getting mad at me." Gun put his head back and closed his eyes again. "I'm not the one who screwed up your love life. What'd you do this time?"

"What makes you think *I* did something?"

Gun merely quirked his eyebrows, and Gabe knew there was no point in attempting to save face. He might as well confess the whole thing. It wasn't as if Gun didn't know—or think he knew—the whole story, anyway, and there was always the chance Gabe would feel better for having vented some of his frustration. Not much of a chance, but at least the possibility was out there. "I kissed her."

That opened the old eyes, Gabe noticed.

"You have had a busy day."

"It happened a year ago, at the Christmas Eve party."

"And it took you until now to figure out you liked it? No wonder she doesn't think much of you. You're not usually so backward, Junior."

"That's not the worst of it. I don't remember."

"You don't...?" The corner of Gun's mouth lifted with rueful comprehension. "You don't remember the kiss."

"I remember waking up on Christmas morning and thinking that Louisa's eggnog recipe ought to be our country's ultimate secret weapon. But that's about the extent of my recall. On the other hand, every time I saw her in the building this past year, I felt like there was something familiar about her.''

''But you didn't do anything to find out what?''

Gabe rubbed the back of his neck. ''She hasn't been what I call approachable, Dad. She never even looked at me sideways when I'd see her across the lobby or in the elevator, always kept her chin up and her eyes straight. You know I'm basically a shy person...I just thought she wasn't interested.''

''So how did you—being the shy, backward person you are—find out you'd kissed this apparently unapproachable woman?''

''She told me. Just blurted it right out.'' He frowned. ''Then she told me to forget it.''

''Hmm... Let's see if I understand the chain of events here.'' Gun strummed his inch-long beard with his finger. ''You drank a few glasses of Christmas cheer, kissed this woman and promptly forgot about it. A year later, she still remembers, you still don't, but now you want to and she's saying forget it.''

''I haven't been able to think of anything else since she told me. Something happens to me when I look at her, Dad, and— Don't even start to say what you're thinking, because it's not like that at all. It's not about sex.... Well, yes, it is, but there's more to it than that. I just don't know what. And now it looks like I'm not going to get the chance to find out.''

''How does that make you a jackass?''

''I don't know,'' he said with a disgruntled shrug.

But the truth was, he did. *Are you a* real *Jack Kass?* the twins had asked. They trusted him, and he was going to let them down. Getting up, he walked to the window again and stood looking out at the snow. "Do you think it's possible she just doesn't like me?"

Gun put his hands behind his head and settled more comfortably in the chair. "Either that or it was a lousy kiss to begin with."

Gabe couldn't believe he was even discussing this. No matter what it was he felt for Katherine...and he was by no means sure it wasn't just a heavy dose of lust...he had no business getting involved with her. No matter how much she intrigued him. No matter how much he liked her kids...and no one could be more surprised about that than he was...it had scared him senseless when they announced to the world outside of Saks's windows that he was their— Well, there was no need even to think about it. He wasn't going to see them again. Or Katherine. He certainly wasn't going to kiss her...much as the idea appealed to him. And he wasn't going to help the twins find Santa Claus, even if he had promised he would. "You know, Dad, it's none of my business how Katherine raises her kids. If she doesn't think they need to believe in Santa Claus, then who am I to say they should?"

Gun's salt-and-pepper brows angled thoughtfully. "Correct me if I'm wrong, Junior, but as I recall, even in the original Christmas story there was a small role for a jackass."

Gabe made no answer. He just watched the snow

come down in thick flurries…and wondered if Katherine was watching it, too.

"This woman…" Gun said. "This…Katherine. How tall is she?"

"It doesn't matter, Dad, because I'm not going to see her again."

Gun nodded as if he understood perfectly. "It was just a thought, Junior. Just a thought."

GRETEL, the magazine's art director, stopped in Katherine's office on her way down the hall. "Where's Janeen?" she asked as she tried to deliver the single message slip, which perched atop the double stack of photos in her arms, by sliding it off without dislodging the entire load. "She hasn't been here all morning, and I'm not sure *Contemporary Woman* magazine should have a man filling in at the reception desk and answering the phone. That may be the modern thing to do, but, Katherine, think of the typos."

Katherine laughed. "John seems to be doing very well, so far. I haven't had a single complaint. Of course, I told him I wasn't really here, no matter who wanted to talk to me. I'd only planned to stay long enough to unearth an article no one else could seem to find, but one thing led to another, and…" She glanced at her watch and groaned. "Tell me it's not twelve-thirty," she said. "I told Janeen I'd be back by eleven."

Gretel slanted the photos at an angle, and the message slip drifted toward the desk. "So what did you do with Janeen? Leave her double-parked?"

"Worse than that. I asked her to baby-sit."

"Oooh, a fate worse than driving in New York traffic." Gretel rebalanced her load of pictures and headed for the door. "Wish you'd asked me. You know how much I enjoy entertaining your kids."

"Exactly why I asked Janeen. That and the fact she was the one who called me to come into the office in the first place." Katherine picked up the slip from her desk and skimmed it.

Janeen called. Santa spotted. Tav'n on Green. 12:30. G.H. sure U wdn't mind.

Frowning, Katherine read John's shorthand again, her pulse snapping in her veins like Mexican jumping beans. She lowered the slip, then abruptly raised it again and reread the message.

"You look ready to set something on fire," Gretel observed. "What did John misspell?"

Reaching for the phone, Katherine punched in the direct-dial to her apartment, even though she already knew no one would answer. They were at the restaurant…Janeen, the twins, and G.H., alias Gaberson Housley, alias the only man in the world who honestly thought she wouldn't *mind!* "Murder," she said tightly. "He's going to have to learn how to spell murder."

TAVERN ON THE GREEN was nestled in Central Park like a flashy piece of costume jewelry on a matron's ample bosom. There was always a crowd, for the only thing more appealing than the food served was the restaurant's decor. Bright, fun and friendly, Tavern on the Green was a popular tourist attraction, and reservations weren't easy to come by at this time of year.

Not that Katherine believed for a moment that Gabe had had any difficulty getting a table at the last minute. He probably played poker with every second waiter in the place. Or provided security guards to safeguard the chef's recipes. Or knew someone who knew someone who wanted to meet Michael Bolton.

She'd worked her way past indignation, ignored a singing sense of anticipation at the battle ahead of her, and was well into quietly furious by the time the cab pulled up outside the restaurant at ten minutes after one. He wasn't going to get away with this, she thought, as she paid the fare and raced under the green canvas canopy to enter the restaurant.

There was such a crowd in the foyer, so many people waiting to be seated, that it took several endless minutes to reach the hostess and then at least five more before someone was found to show her the way to Mr. Housley's table. Helen Gurley Brown nodded from her seat in an alcove of the restaurant, and there were a handful of other professional acquaintances who acknowledged Katherine's passing with a wave or a few words of seasonal greetings. But she didn't waver in her purpose. At least, she didn't until she caught sight of Gabe.

He was sitting at a table next to the long wall of windows. On either side of him, Andy and Abby were kneeling in their respective chairs, leaning across the table with their chins propped on their hands, their rapt attention on something beyond Katherine's range of vision. Across from them, Janeen had turned her chair around so that she, too, could see outside. But it was Gabe's expression that stopped her, there in the narrow passage between two tables.

On one level, she noticed that his persistently stubborn lock of hair drooped casually toward his forehead, as if he'd recently brushed it back and it was just awaiting an unsuspecting moment to fall forward again. And she was vaguely conscious that he was wearing a striped long-sleeved polo shirt that had just the right amount of material to fit smoothly across his shoulders and chest and around his well-toned arms without appearing too tight or too loose. The collar was white—she noted that inane detail only because it made such a contrast against his tan. But it wasn't even the combination of those appealing factors that stopped her in her tracks. Oh, no, nothing in her life could be that simple.

It was the look on his face as he watched Abby's and Andy's obvious delight in whatever had captured their interest outside. Gabe appeared mesmerized by them and when they laughed aloud—not the giggles and high-pitched squeals they usually rendered, but the throaty, translucent tones of pure joy that only children seemed capable of producing—he looked from one to the other with such a mix of enjoyment and flat-out bewilderment that Katherine's heart went out to him. Not because he liked her children, but because he was so obviously flabbergasted that he did.

"Excuse me, please." A waiter paused behind her, and Katherine realized she was blocking his way.

"Oh, sorry," she said, and stepped aside so he could pass. As the waiter moved on, Gabe looked up and saw her. If the slant of his smile hadn't leaped across the room to reach her, she might have held on to the righteous indignation that had brought her this far. If he hadn't looked so happy to see her, so damned *pleased* by the simple fact of her presence, maybe she could have managed a face-saving aggravation.

But he rose, slowly pushing back his chair, the warmth in his whiskey-brown eyes welcoming her even before she was close enough to take a seat. Which she had had no intention of doing, but which now seemed imperative. The wobbly feeling at the backs of her knees did not bode well for remaining upright. She managed to traverse the space between them without losing her balance, but the moment he reached across and touched her hand, she felt the impact of attraction all the way to her toes and knew she'd better sit...immediately, if not sooner.

"Katherine," he said, his voice flowing over her like raw silk warmed in the sun. "I didn't expect to see you here." He pulled up another chair, snatching it away from the nearest table without asking permission from the couple seated there. With great chivalry, he scooted the chair close to his and held it as she gratefully sank onto its sturdiness, all the while wondering what had happened to the cool and perfectly justified anger she had felt only a moment before. What in the world was wrong, when just the look in a man's eyes could knock the stuffing right out of her? She was darn lucky he wasn't wearing his coat, or she'd have been toast—with butter—right then and there.

"Hi, Mom." Andy spared her a glance before resuming his rapt gaze out the window. "Santa Claus is throwing reindeer."

"And presents," Abby added without breaking her concentration.

"Hi, Katherine. Isn't he good?" Janeen scooted back her chair, to allow an unobscured view of the garden outside, and of the juggler who was dressed like Santa and who was tossing stuffed reindeer and various wrapped packages into the air with apparent ease.

"I don't know how long he can keep up the show, but they've been fascinated since he started." Gabe nodded at the twins. "And still. I didn't think they knew how to sit so still."

She leaned toward Gabe, being cautious not to get too close. "I'm furious with you," she whispered, hoping that the act of saying the words would reignite the feeling. "Absolutely furious."

"Good," he whispered back. "I always prefer it when women feel passionately toward me."

Annoyance made a quarter turn inside her. "This is first cousin to kidnapping, you know."

He leaned nearer, bringing the tantalizing scent of his cologne and the subtle aroma of cinnamon and coffee with him. "No relationship at all," he said. "I'm here completely of my own free will."

Feeling more irritated by the moment, Katherine

brought her commanding gaze to the man who had caused her to lose a lot more sleep last night than Abby's half hour of upset stomach. "I asked you to stay out of our lives."

Gabe took in the sparkle in her eyes, the high angle of her chin, the tenseness in her shoulders, the flush of excitement on her cheeks, and decided that whatever she was afraid of in him, she was equally enamored of. "I know you did, Katherine, and I thought about it. But I just don't see that happening."

"You don't see..." She started repeating his statement, as if she must have misunderstood, then turned more fully toward him, the light of battle in her stormy eyes. "Well, do you see yourself being slapped with a restraining order?" she asked. "Because that's beginning to look like a distinct possibility."

Gabe decided this was the show to watch. Kate had the juggler beat all to pieces. "There's no need to get so upset just because I can't remember kissing you."

She opened her mouth to refute that, but nothing came out, and she ended up just staring at him for a minute. "That has nothing to do with this," she finally said.

"I think it does. I think that's what all of this is about."

"Well, it isn't," she snapped, but there was a note of distraction in her voice now. "I'm sorry I ever even told you about that. Forget it."

Gabe put his lips so close to her ear he almost

singed his lips on her furious blush. "Kissing you is all I can think about."

She pulled back so fast he thought she would fall out of the chair. "But you can't. That's...impossible. You don't remember anything about it."

"Doesn't stop me from thinking, Kate. Doesn't stop me from imagining what it was like, how it felt. You've remembered that one kiss for a year," he pointed out. "Next time I won't forget...not a single detail. You can count on it."

She gulped. He heard her. "There won't be a next—"

"Oh, look!" Janeen's exclamation drew Katherine's attention, but Gabe was slower to follow her gaze to the entertainment on the other side of the window. His eyes lingered on her, his thoughts centered on the tight feeling in his chest. He'd dated plenty of women, been infatuated a thousand times, and imagined himself in love one time too many. But he'd never known a woman who he believed was so infatuated with him...and so desperately determined not to be. He could no more walk away from that mystery than everyone around him could keep from smiling as the Santa Claus juggler stopped tossing inanimate objects to comically scratch a visible, moving itch in his heavily padded belly.

When a small black head poked out, the juggler mimed astonishment, and Andy turned to look, wide-eyed, at Gabe. "It's a monkey! Look! He's got a monkey in his suit!"

Applause spattered around them, and the diners returned to their meals as the red-suited juggler put the monkey on his shoulder and began gathering up his props.

"I knew it was a monkey," Abby announced as she slid down into her seat. "And I knew he wasn't the *real* Santa the minute I saw him." She arched an accusing eyebrow at Gabe. "You said Santa Claus was going to be here, so where is he?"

"I said I *heard* he was spotted in Central Park," Gabe explained easily. "Maybe he's at Wollman Rink."

"Ice-skating?" Abby sat straight, interest written all over her face.

"He's too fat to ice-skate." Andy took his fork and began to spear green beans without mercy. "Hey, Mom, guess what? Gabe eats snails. I watched him."

"We're not going ice-skating." Katherine scooted her chair an infinitesimal degree away from Gabe's. "We're going to the museum."

Janeen picked up her purse. "Guess it's time I headed back to the office."

"Mom, please, can't we go ice-skating?"

"Snails are slimy slugs, and Gabe ate a whole bunch of 'em."

"Thanks for lunch, Gabe."

"My pleasure," he answered Janeen, wondering how he could persuade Katherine to spend the afternoon with him, wondering if he could ever be alone with her.

"Don't you like slimy snails, Gabe?" Andy had been furtively sliding green beans off his plate and onto the floor all during lunch, but now he'd changed tactics and skewered the leftovers onto his fork. Gabe kept an eye on him, figuring it was only a matter of time before he fired them across the table at Abby.

"I do," Gabe said. "I like snails. Uh, Katherine, does Janeen have to go back to the office?"

"Yes. No. Why?"

"If she takes the twins to the rink, I could take you to the museum." He tried to make it sound logical, a simple solution to a perplexing problem, but he could see she wasn't going to buy it. "Wouldn't that be all right with you guys?" He turned to the twins, counting on their enthusiasm.

"Yes!" Abby bounded up to throw her arms around Janeen's knees, lest she get away. "Please, please, please, Janeen! Take us, please. I'll teach you to ice-skate. I'm real good at it."

"Well, I..." Janeen looked to Katherine for instructions.

"I don't want to go to no dumb museum." Andy tilted the tines of the fork forward, testing his aim.

"*Any* dumb museum," Katherine corrected, turning to Gabe. "And thank you, but no, thank you. We're going to go to the museum."

"All right. We'll all go to the museum." Putting his hands at her waist, he moved her aside and reached around her to scuttle the launch of the green-bean missile.

"Hey!" Andy frowned as Gabe lifted the loaded fork and set it aside. "I was gonna eat those."

"*I want to go ice-skating!*" Abby's plaintive protest ended in tears. "Please, Mom, let Janeen take me ice-skating."

Katherine looked lost, suddenly, and Gabe picked up his coat, motioning to the twins to get theirs. "You're coming with me," he told Katherine. "They're going to the rink with Janeen. No arguments."

To his amazement, there wasn't one.

But only because Janeen slipped on a green bean and sprained her ankle.

Chapter Eight

Gabe draped his arm around the back of the spectators' bench and wished he'd brought his other coat. "Are you warm enough?"

"Fine." Katherine huddled next to him, her scarf looped twice around her neck, her chin burrowed into its wooly warmth, her gloved hands forming a pocket of insulation around a foam cup. Steam escaped from a slit in the lid and wafted upward, laden with the aroma of hot coffee. "They're bound to get tired of being out in this cold pretty soon."

Gabe looked across the ice, easily locating the neon pink and purple parkas amid the multicolored bundles skating round and round Wollman Rink. From where he and Katherine sat on the row of benches in the parents' gallery, he couldn't see the twins' expressions, but he'd have bet a hundred dollars they weren't feeling the cold. From the way they were skating, darting awkwardly first toward, then away from each other, it was obvious to him that they were playing tag, and expending a lot of healthy energy to do it, too. "They don't look cold," he said and Katherine sighed, her breath escaping in a visible puff. "You can wait inside, if you want," he offered. "I'll watch them."

She shook her head. "You don't have to stay, you know."

"Oh, I think I do. After all, I'm the one who told them Santa would be here."

Katherine's eyes cut to his face, then returned to the twins as they rounded the far curve. "I thought we agreed you'd call off this ridiculous quest to find the *real* Santa Claus."

"I don't believe that's what *we* agreed at all."

"I'm angry with you for taking the twins out today without my permission."

He nodded, acknowledging her right to the emotion. "Janeen did call the office to ask you if it would be okay."

"She left a message which said, 'G.H. was sure you wouldn't mind,' which is not the same as asking."

"She told me you didn't care."

"And you believed her?"

He felt it was only fair that he admit some culpability in the deception. "I figured that at some point in the conversation you had said the actual words *I don't care.* I just chose to accept Janeen's interpretation that it was all right with you. But I didn't know she hadn't talked to you at all."

"Don't do it again, Gabe."

He turned toward her, taking note of her seriousness. "You weren't worried, were you?"

Her lips tightened. "If it had been anyone other

than you and Janeen, I'd have been angry *and* terrified.''

"I never thought of it like that." He was honestly surprised that he hadn't. "I'm always so conscious of security, I just assumed you knew they'd be safe with me."

"If I didn't believe that, you wouldn't be sitting here with me, now." She raised the cup and blew softly on the steam. "But that isn't to say I'm ready to give you carte blanche to drop by anytime you feel like it and take them out to lunch."

Gabe was pleased beyond reason that she trusted him, flattered that she did so intuitively, and suddenly terribly conscious of the responsibility of that trust. "I'm sorry, Katherine. I didn't even stop to think about it from your perspective. It won't happen again."

"No, it won't."

He decided to ignore the implications of that. It was one thing to be sorry because he had caused her to worry, another thing entirely to bow politely out of the picture just because he worried her. "From now on," he said conversationally, "you'll know everything I'm going to do up-front."

"That's a comfort," she said dryly.

"Mom! Gabe! Look at us!" Andy waved as he and Abby skated past, their padded arms jerking up and down for balance, as if they were walking a tightrope instead of a solid sheet of ice.

"Isabelle Kinser skates with the Junior Olympians," Katherine remarked pensively, her gaze following the twins as their legs scissored forward and back with unskilled but highly enthusiastic precision. Gabe watched their progress with more pride than he had ever taken in his own ability to zip around the rink chasing a hockey puck.

"Isabelle Kinser is going to grow up to be a snob, no matter how well she can skate," he observed.

"So, you're saying I should be happy my children won't have the same opportunities as Isabelle to become snobs."

"I'm saying Isabelle Kinser hasn't a hope of ever reaching the level of self-worth that Abby and Andy already possess."

She sighed heavily. "I guess her lower level of self-worth would be why Isabelle's in school right now and Abby and Andy are suspended." Katherine sipped her coffee. "I really should have insisted they spend the afternoon at the museum."

"What for?"

"Because they might learn something?" she suggested with a touch of sarcasm. "Because since they're not in school, they ought to be spending their afternoon doing something a little less fun and a little more educational?"

"Who says ice-skating isn't educational?" he challenged. "Look at them. They're out there on the ice having fun and learning things you couldn't pound into their heads in school or a museum."

"Like what? The law of gravity?"

He grinned. "They appear to be absorbing that one from the bottom up. But just think of all the other hands-on experience they're getting in physics...the theory of relativity, the principles of momentum and resistance.''

"I don't know about the theory of relativity, but they were born knowing about momentum and resistance. Any other bright ideas on what scientific principles they're absorbing out there?''

"Well, they're exploring the theory that an object set in motion, tends to stay in motion.''

"Mmm...sounds iffy to me, unless the discovery would be that an ice-skater, once set in motion, can only be stopped by resistance, gravity, or the toe of her brother's ice skate.''

He laughed. "See, I told you, they're getting a well-rounded education right here at Wollman Rink.''

"A well-*grounded* one, at any rate. Still, I can't help but think I'm rewarding them for bad behavior.''

"I think if anyone's being rewarded for bad behavior, it's you.''

"Me? What have I done?''

"You hung up on me, for one thing.''

"I did not.''

"You did, and you also made certain I couldn't sleep last night.''

"I don't see how you can hold me responsible for your inability to sleep.''

He let his eyes answer, let his glance slide to her lips, let her own memory of their once-upon-a-time kiss rise to accuse her.

She lifted her chin in denial. "That seductive gaze

may work beautifully on women who know how to *purr,* Gabe, but I'm not one of them."

He shrugged, satisfied by the defensiveness in her response. "Ah, well, purring is overrated, in my humble opinion. Unless, of course, it comes from a cat. Have you ever given any thought to trading Abby's stuffed lion for a kitten?"

Turning her head, she frowned at him with all the fierceness of a lioness. "No, I haven't, and I don't intend to, either. I don't care if she did tell you that story about Matilda being a real kitten before a wicked witch—who just happens to look like me, as Abby loves to point out—turned her into a raggedy toy lion. We are not getting a kitten."

"Obviously a sore point. I suppose, there's no need to even ask about Sparky, the dog?"

"Imaginary," she informed him. "Sparky, the *imaginary* dog. And that's the way I intend for him to stay, too."

"You don't like animals."

"I do like animals," she said on a sigh. "But an apartment in the city is no place for one. I can't take on the responsibility of a pet...the feeding, walking, training, walking, watering and, of course, walking. And don't even suggest I could hire one of those pet-care services. I just don't see the point."

"Can I bring my dog to visit?" he asked, although he didn't own a dog and wasn't sure he remembered how to operate one.

"Is he obedience-trained?"

Gabe tried for an offended look. "His manners are impeccable...like his master's."

"Then I suppose it might be all right. Once. Abby and Andy would love it, but I'll warn you now, they'll bounce off the wall with excitement, so you may want to give the poor dog a tranquilizer before you come."

"I'll do that," he agreed with a smile, wondering when it would hit her that she had just invited him over.

"Hey, Mom!" Abby yelled from some distance back. "Watch me! I'm going to do a spin!"

Katherine started to rise in protest, but Gabe laid his hand on her shoulder and she stayed put. "Let her try," he said. "The worst that can happen is she'll—"

She fell flat on her behind, but she was scrambling to her feet in the next instant, ready to try again. "Look, Mom! I'm in the Ice Capades!"

Katherine settled back and took another sip of coffee. "I guess I tend to be a little overprotective," she said.

"Understandable." Gabe left his hand on her shoulder, liking the protective feeling it gave him, liking the way she hadn't shrugged it off. "You're very brave, Kate. I'm awed by your decision to become a single mother. It couldn't have been an easy choice to make."

"If that's another way of saying I certainly chose a roundabout, complicated way to get pregnant, then I guess I'd agree it was a brave thing to do. At the time, I just knew I wanted to have a child and I didn't want anyone else involved in my decision."

"No man wanting to be a daddy, in other words."

"Or not wanting to be, which would have been worse."

"Having been raised by my dad, that's a little hard for me to imagine."

She looked at him curiously. "Your mother?"

"She died when I was five. I remember things…a voice, a touch, laughter…but I don't really remember her."

Katherine was silent, then, and Gabe didn't press her. He knew she must be considering all the memories the twins would never have of the father they would never know. On the ice, Andy, being a brother, laughed hysterically as Abby attempted another spin and promptly landed on her butt, for at least the third time in the past five minutes. Gabe smiled, thinking Abby was every bit as determined, and on her way to being just as brave, as her mother.

"My father left when I was eight," Katherine said, surprising Gabe with the suddenness of the confession. "He left right before Christmas. He made this elaborate plan to meet my mother and me at Macy's so I could sit on Santa's lap and we could do the Christmas shopping together, but then he never showed up. Turns out, he just wanted us out of the house so he could pack his things."

She met Gabe's eyes, but while there was a curve on her lips, there wasn't a trace of a smile. "My mother tried to pretend he'd be back. She even went so far as to tell me Santa Claus needed Daddy's help at the North Pole and he'd be home on Christmas morning. But I knew it was a lie. I only saw him once after that…at my mother's funeral, ten years ago. He brought his new wife and their teenaged daughter. She was very pretty." Katherine shrugged, as if the pain were too old to bother her anymore. "He seemed happy to see me, but I haven't heard from him since."

"I'm sorry." Gabe could hardly get the words out over the ache in his throat. "What an awful thing to have happen to you."

"Yes." She lifted her cup, but didn't drink, just held its warmth against her lips. "I haven't told anyone that pitiful story in ages." Her glance slid to him, then away. "Just goes to show how hard I'm trying to warn you away."

"And I thought you were just being nice, giving me an excuse to tell you my own sad stories."

Her mouth softened in sympathy. "Having your mother die when you're only five is pretty sad. I hope you don't have many stories sadder than that one."

He wanted to take her in his arms and hold her until she couldn't remember how it felt to be sad, how it felt to know your father had deserted you to make a new family, a new daughter. But that was more comfort than he knew how to offer, more than she knew how to accept. So he cleared his throat and offered the only cure he knew for sadness. "If we're going to be swapping pitiful stories, I should probably warn you I've got some that will have you sobbing into your beer...er, coffee. And in this weather, that may require a can of deicer."

She made a melancholy attempt at a smile. "I'll take my chances. Go ahead. Do your worst. Tell me something horrible that happened to you."

His arm moved easily around her, cupping her against his side in a companionable fit. She didn't pull away, which pretty much made his day. "It's difficult for me to talk about this without choking up," he began somberly. "But, well, once I asked Santa for a pony, and—"

She interrupted with a nudge of her elbow in his ribs. "You already told me that story, and it wasn't horrible."

"It wasn't?"

"No, you asked Santa for a pony, but you got a dog, instead."

"Oh, that's right. I forgot."

"And you're supposed to have such an *excellent* memory, too."

"Well, give me a minute to think about it. I'm positive I have some other angst-ridden story locked inside me, somewhere. Oh, I know. I've got it. There was the time Dad got shot…in the butt…with a BB gun. *My* BB gun, to be specific. The one Santa brought. Now, that was a terrible experience. And it happened on Christmas Day, too, so instead of getting to play with my new BB gun and shoot the devil out of a paper target, I had to spend the entire afternoon in the emergency room with a very cranky father."

Laughter lit a sparkle in her eyes, and her lips curved in a frown that somehow looked very much like a smile. And Gabe felt like he'd just gotten the only Christmas present he ever wanted.

"Can we walk home through the Park, Gabe?" Andy asked almost the second Katherine got his skates off. The apartment building was only a few blocks away, and she'd already decided the walk would be a good way for the twins to wind down from their exhilarating hour on the ice rink. But to have the question put to Gabe so naturally, as if it were his decision to make, caught her off guard.

"You'll have to ask your mother." Gabe smoothly deferred to her authority, and she just as smoothly agreed that a walk through Central Park would be the perfect way to get home.

But the moment lingered in her mind, Andy's innocent question taking on significance as she strolled beside Gabe down one of the paved paths. She had let down her guard, let the twins become too comfortable with him. She had no idea how she'd come to do that. She only knew she couldn't let it continue.

"I thought they'd be exhausted by now," he said in a tone of wonder.

Katherine followed his gaze, making sure the twins weren't dashing too far ahead in their race to pack a thousand activities into a thirty-minute walk. "That *is* exhaustion for a seven-year-old."

"That? You mean, they get tired and they go faster?"

"Faster, louder, funnier, everything magnified twice over. They'll fight sleep tooth and nail tonight."

"I'm exhausted just thinking about it."

"Maybe you should go home now and take a nap."

He grinned. "And admit I have no stamina? No,

thank you. Besides, you'll need me if a question about biology comes up on this little nature hike.''

"It's only physics I'm a little fuzzy about. I think I can handle biology.''

"Mom!" Abby shouted. "Over here! Look what Andy found!"

"I hope it's a spider's nest," Gabe said as he headed for the spot where the twins had clustered.

Spiders? Come to think of it, she didn't know all that much about biology and, really, there was no reason Gabe shouldn't walk them all the way home.

THERE really was no reason not to invite him up to the apartment for a cup of coffee, either. After all, when they finally reached the co-op building and entered the lobby, he was just as rosy from the cold as she and the twins were, and it seemed churlish to send him immediately back out into the weather again.

"Hey, Gabe!" Andy's eyes brightened with inspiration. "Wanna come up to our 'partment and play Jet Jupiter, Laser Ranger, with me and Abby?''

"I get the big pan for my helmet," Abby shouted, and raced for the bank of elevators.

"That's *my* helmet, Abby!" Andy took off after her.

Gabe looked after them, then turned toward Katherine, a hopeful glint in his brown eyes.

"Do you want to come upstairs and warm up a bit?" she asked. "I could make some coffee."

"I'd like that. Thanks." His words were warm. So was his smile, and she was feeling a little too warm already. Coffee, she decided. One cup. Then she'd show him the door.

"MOM? Is Gabe still here?"

Katherine pulled the covers over Andy's Bugs Bunny pajamas and tucked them around his shoulders. "He's in the kitchen, cleaning up the mess you guys made."

Andy smiled through a huge yawn. "That was the best hot chocolate I ever had, Mom. Only I wish it could have been strawberry hot chocolate. That would be good, wouldn't it?"

"Delicious."

"Gabe is good at making delicious. I liked how he cooked dinner. Tyler's dad cooks moo goo gai pan. Tyler told me. I wonder if Gabe knows how to cook that. Aren't you glad he stayed and cooked for us and watched *The Muppets Christmas Carol* with us and made us hot chocolate? Aren't you glad me and Abby ask'd him to?"

"Abby and I," she corrected, unwilling to admit even to herself how glad she was that Gabe had stayed. Because if she admitted that she had enjoyed the evening as much as the twins had, it would be harder to say to Gabe what had to be said. Tonight. Face-to-face.

"Could you maybe ask him to come and say goodnight to me again?"

"No, Andy, I couldn't."

"But, Mom, I forgot to tell him something."

She gave her son a meaningful look. "I'll be glad to tell him for you, but he has to go home, now,

Andy. And you have to go to sleep. No more getting out of bed tonight.''

"I haven't got out of bed since the first time you tucked me in," he announced indignantly. "Is Abby asleep yet?"

"I don't know. Why don't you be the first one asleep tonight?"

"I'm too excited, Mom. I can't wait to see the North Pole."

Katherine frowned, separating a strand of truth from the many threads of his imagination. "Are you planning to dream about the North Pole?"

He shook his head vigorously against the pillow. "It's not a dream, Mom. Gabe's takin' me on Saturday. He said."

"Taking you where?"

"To the North Pole," Andy explained with exaggerated patience. "He said since we couldn't find the *real* Santa Claus here, we were just gonna have to go look for him at the North Pole. At his workshop."

"Whose workshop?"

Andy rolled his eyes. "Santa's. Weren't ya listenin'?"

"I think someone forgot to say anything to me about this. When did Gabe mention it?"

"When he came in to say good-night. Ask Abby. He told her, too."

She smoothed back the red-gold curls from his forehead. "And how, Mr. I-Haven't-Been-Out-of-Bed, do you know he told her, too?"

He rounded his eyes innocently, a sure sign of

guilt. "She came in my room, Mom. I didn't go in her room. I didn't. Really."

Leaning down to give him a kiss, Katherine straightened and walked to the door. "This is the last tuck-in, Andrew. Don't get out of bed again tonight."

"Okay, Mom. I won't. Good night, Mom."

"Good night, Andy."

"I love you."

"I love you." Pulling the door partly closed, she stepped across the hall to say another, and hopefully final, good-night to Abby. But Abby was already asleep, her eyelashes curving against her cheeks in a thick, gold shadow, her squiggly curls strewn all around her face in a riotous freedom from the braids she'd worn all day. Katherine kissed her, too, and smoothed the covers around her thin shoulders.

"Mom?"

Andy called her as she left Abby's room, and she opened his door and looked in. "I thought we'd already said good-night," she reminded him.

"I have to ask Gabe somethin' important, Mom. Please? I'll just ask him one thing, then I promise I'll go right to sleep."

She sighed, uncomfortable that in such a short amount of time, Gabe Housley had woven his way into their routine. Even if it was only one night. Even if it never happened again. It had been too easily accomplished this once, and that was what bothered her most. "You can ask me, Andy. I'm sure I can answer any question you have. I've always answered them before, haven't I?"

There was hesitation in the semi-darkness. "It's a *guy* question, Mom. Couldn't I please ask Gabe?"

It's a guy *question,* she repeated to herself as she looked at him, sitting up in bed, Bugs Bunny glowing in the dark on his pajama top. How did they learn this so young? she wondered. How did they know there was *guy* stuff and *girl* stuff and that it wasn't all the *same* stuff? "I'll ask Gabe to come back so you can ask him one question, Andy, but then you have to go to sleep. I mean it."

He snuggled happily under the covers, once again pulling them up over Bugs Bunny's glowing face. "Okay, Mom. I mean it, too. I'll go to sleep soon's I get to talk to Gabe."

She started to close the door.

"Mom?"

"Yes, Andy?"

"I love you."

"I love you, too."

KATHERINE stood by the window, waiting for Gabe to return from his question-and-answer session with Andy. As soon as he did, she was going to have it out with him.

Well, maybe that was too strong a term for the matter-of-fact discussion she had in mind. Conversation, really. There wasn't anything to be discussed. She was simply going to tell him that she wasn't interested in having a relationship. If he pressed for an explanation, she'd tell him it was nothing personal, just a decision she'd made to keep her life, and the lives of her children, a little less complicated.

And it wasn't as if the three of them needed anyone else. She'd considered all the angles and made peace with the sacrifices before she ever got pregnant. She'd made her choices, and she was sticking with them. And that was why she didn't have relationships with men.

She had fantasies. Harmless, uncomplicated fantasies that didn't make demands, didn't have expectations, didn't get up some morning, pack a suitcase and head for higher ground. Fantasies were easy, available, and completely within her control.

But of course she wouldn't tell him that. She wouldn't blurt out the embarrassing admission that she had been carrying on a most satisfying fantasy with him for nearly a year. Ever since the kiss he didn't remember. Actually, even before that...since the first time she'd seen him in the lobby of the Fitzpatrick Building, wearing that Armani coat. He wore it for her, occasionally, in the fantasy, but somehow, she could never get him out of it, couldn't get him to be the flasher she had in mind. Now that she thought about it, he had been very coy lately—with or without the coat—and he had not been all that cooperative. And as to satisfying... Well, once she convinced the flesh and blood Gabe to stay out of her life, she would turn her attention to whipping the fantasy Gabe into shape.

A self-conscious blush heated her cheeks. Well, she wasn't into whipping, but she just might start insisting that he unbutton that coat when she told him to. But that was all for later on. Right now, she needed to focus on what she wanted to say to him.

Taking a deep breath, she focused…and wondered how he'd look in nothing but his Calvin Kleins. No, wait. Focus. She wasn't interested in a relationship. Good. That was good. Focus on what she wanted to say. She wasn't interested in having a relationship with him. No, she was interested in having sex with him.

This was not good. Not good at all.

Another deep breath shoved the fantasy into the closet. Another one brought the room, the view, the coming conversation, into sharp focus. She was calm, cool, collected, a stranger to impulse, a strong, decisive woman, who knew what she wanted and was completely impervious to the appeal of his warm quirk of a smile.

The kitchen light went out, and her calm fled, just from the knowledge that he was on the way. Then the dining room lights went out and her stomach did a swan dive, taking cool and collected with it. Then he walked across the living room toward her, switching off one lamp, and then another, until the only light left on was the forty-watt halogen in the corner and her strong, decisive inner woman suddenly became very chummy with the impulse to throw herself at him and start ripping off his clothes.

"Do you have something against the electric company?" she asked, because she had to say something.

"It's habit. Dad goes around the house turning on the lights and I go around turning them off."

Her eyes adjusted to the softer light, but he continued to move toward her, and she began a life-and-death struggle with the impulse. "You, uh, live with your dad?"

"He lives with me…when he's not out making the world a safer place for the good guys. He thinks he's Spenser for Hire nine days out of ten."

"Who is he on the tenth day?" She would get this breathing problem under control…no matter how many inane remarks she had to make.

"Sometimes he's Lieutenant Columbo. Sometimes, James Bond." Gabe came to a stop a bare three feet from where she stood, and she had to clasp her hands behind her. "I've even accused him of being Miss Marple, at times. But he's a good detective. A good man." Gabe smiled. "He'd like you. You're short."

She blinked and congratulated herself on taking a nonchalant step away from him. "I…don't think I'll be meeting your dad. In fact, I'm afraid I won't be seeing you again, either."

"You'll see me tomorrow. I thought we'd take the kids to see the Christmas show at Radio City Music Hall. Not that I believe the *real* Santa Claus will be there, but I think they'll enjoy it."

"Of course they will, Gabe. They're having such a good time, they're practically drowning in enjoyment."

"You almost make it sound like a bad thing." He took a step closer. "But I'm drowning in enjoyment, too, and I can tell you it's good."

She was in trouble here. She knew by the low, husky, seductive tone of his voice. She knew by the heated awareness spiraling through her. She knew by the impulse that leaped to attention in her thoughts. Distraction. She needed a distraction. "What was the question Andy had to ask you before he could go to sleep?"

Gabe did not look distracted. He looked as if he wanted to kiss her. "He wanted to know what snails taste like."

"That's it?" Her eyes drifted to his mouth, but she didn't allow them to linger. "I was imagining all kinds of *guy* things a little boy might want to ask out of earshot of his mother, but 'What do snails taste like?' was not a possibility."

"He wanted to know if they taste like dirt."

"Oh." She was breathless and couldn't keep her glance from falling to his lips. "Do they?"

"They taste like earthworms, only chewier."

"I hope you were just using your imagination when you said that."

He raised his hand and ran his fingers through her hair, watching as it fell in strands of flyaway gold against her cheek. Then he gathered the feathered tendrils and tucked them, like a flower, behind her ear. "I'm using my imagination now," he said softly.

So was she...and feeling darned frustrated doing it, too. "There was something I wanted to...wanted to...say," she began, although she couldn't remember what it could have been. "I wanted to say..."

"Kiss me," he supplied, bringing his hands to cup her shoulders.

"That...wasn't it." Although she was fairly certain she liked his idea better than hers. "We need to...talk. I have something to...to tell you."

"Do you think it could wait?" His gaze traced the tip of her tongue as she moistened her lips, and Katherine was sure she would never breathe normally again. "Because I need to kiss you. And I need to do it very soon."

Her fingers were tingling. Also her toes. It was possible she was tingling all over. "I think it's only fair..." she whispered in soft, breathy syllables "...to tell you I'm not interested in a relationship."

"Okay." He slid his hands down her arms and took possession of her tingling fingers. "Are you interested in an affair?"

"Oh, yeah," she said impulsively, anticipation flaring like the flame of a candle left in an open door. Before he could make another move, she had flung herself into his arms and was on her tiptoes and kissing him full on the mouth. It was just like the time in his office. She hadn't gone there to kiss him, hadn't even had a thought of doing so. But she'd been looking for someone to let her out of the building, and in the dusky darkness, she'd seen Gabe moving toward her and recognized him by his size and the way he moved. And there had been the mistletoe, tied with a silver bow that shone like a guiding star above the doorway he was fast approaching, and somewhere distant she could hear people laughing, and it had been Christmas Eve and she had been going home alone...and in the heat of an overpowering impulse, she had thrown herself into his arms, kissing him with all the pent-up passion anonymity could provide. She had been amazed by her actions—was still amazed that she had done something so uninhibited—and completely mesmerized by the melting response that singular kiss aroused.

And it was happening again. Now. All of it. Except this time he knew who she was. This time, she couldn't pretend it was an accident. Or that she had merely imagined the pure, unadulterated lust that rushed through her veins like lemmings toward the sea.

If he was startled at first, she was too involved in the kiss to notice. But when he slowly, deliberately, eased into control, she paid attention...if only because the sensation of his mouth moving against hers in sensuous nudges was heaven. Then, as if heaven were just the preliminary phase of delight, Gabe proceeded to deepen the embrace, moving his hands to her hips, coaxing her against his thighs, and submerging any protest that dared arise against the obliterating deluge of sensations. Katherine felt her only choice was to follow his lead and, accordingly, her hands slid around his waist and down.

A soft moan of pleasure entered her as his hands moved up and down her back, caressing every pleasure point along her spine, giving each one a special, stimulating attention. Katherine reciprocated, despite the deliciously weak sensation permeating every square inch of her body, up to and including her tingling fingertips.

It wasn't supposed to be like this, she thought. It was supposed to be a mutual thing, a shared exchange of passions...equal passions. He wasn't supposed to be so in control. She wasn't supposed to be so...willing.

She wasn't sure how she came to be lying on the couch a few minutes later. Probably Gabe had suggested it with a touch and she'd promptly thrown herself across the cushions before he had a chance to ask. But when she realized through a haze of sensual pleasure that she was in an awkward...albeit a very gratifying...position on her back, under the mesmerizing command of Gabe's lips...and a good portion of his body... Well, she couldn't just go on pretending she was involved in a nice, safe fantasy.

Not that she'd ever had a fantasy quite this stimulating. Or one she'd been so totally averse to bringing to a climax.

Climax? The single word and its double meaning opened her eyes in a startled blink, and she made a frantic check to ensure she was still in possession of all her clothes. She considered it a good omen when she discovered that the only things missing were her shoes and a good chunk of her pride.

Now, if she could just get off this couch and away from the temptation to drown herself in his kisses, she'd tell him she had no intention of having an affair or of ever seeing him again. His lips nudged hers with gentle persuasion, and she nudged back, because it seemed unnecessary to be abrupt. She'd ease her way out of this. That was what she'd do. She'd stop kissing him first, then she'd put her lips to his ear and tell him there was no hope of this relationship going anywhere fast. Or slow. No. There was no chance of this relationship going nowhere. That was it. Yes, that was what she'd tell him. Just as soon as she figured out why she'd thought she wanted to stop kissing him.

But it wasn't until the kiss fell apart for lack of oxygen that her memory returned a full and embarrassing account of her wants, actions, and intentions. Katherine came to her senses in a heartbeat, sitting straight up and pulling Gabe up with her. "That's not the way this was supposed to happen," she said, in a voice that mimicked her tenuous control and the rapid cadence of her pulse.

He moved into a sitting position beside her, draping his arm around her shoulders and moving into her space again, into the danger zone. "Show me how it *was* supposed to happen, Kate, and I'll try again."

"No." Her hands were at his chest, her fingers curling with the longing to unbutton the placket and jerk the shirt over his head and off. She couldn't quite get her fingers to move off his chest, but at least she was holding her own with the buttons. "No. We are going nowhere with this."

"Define nowhere," he said, his breath caressing the hollows of her throat, his lips suggesting that if she would only lift her chin just a little, he would be able to caress more of her.

"Nowhere," she whispered, lifting her chin and letting her head fall back against his arm. His kisses nibbled away at her reason. "Nowhere... That would be...where this is going."

"Mmm..." he murmured as he kissed his way along the curve of her throat until he reached her lips. "I've never wanted to go nowhere before."

"Me either."

His kisses requested her silence then, with a sensuous, slow, and tender touch. A series of touches, really. Gliding from one corner of her mouth to the other. Her lips parted, inviting the scintillating appeal of his tongue, anticipating a new onslaught of pleasures...pleasures that failed to materialize when he abruptly pulled back and scooted a short distance away from her. When he turned his head and looked into her eyes, her heart nearly melted from the heat of desire in his gaze. "Much as I hate to say this," he said. "This is as close to going nowhere as we can get, tonight. I didn't come prepared for this, and while I'd like to think you are, I have a strong hunch you're not."

She frowned, confused as much by the overwhelming yearning to be in his arms as by whatever he was trying to tell her. "Prepared? I'm not even coherent."

His smile made her tingle all over again, and she folded her hands firmly in her lap. "I think it's time you went home."

"I think you're right." He stood and reached for her hand, tried to pry one from the other, and finally grasped them both and drew her to her feet. "You can walk me to the door," he suggested.

Yes. She could do that without completely embarrassing herself, she thought. "Okay." Her legs felt shaky, but she congratulated herself on moving steadily, decisively, ahead of Gabe toward the door. When she opened it and turned to him, he paused expectantly. "I don't think I should kiss you again," she said quickly. "Really, I think you should go."

His eyes smiled in amusement. "I'm going. As soon as I get my coat."

"Oh, your coat." She was feeling stronger by the minute. He was just waiting for his coat. Good. She'd get it for him. Opening the coat closet, she pulled it off a hanger and handed it to him. "There," she said with a smile. "Your coat."

"Thank you." He looped the wool scarf about his neck first, then slipped into the coat and reached into his pockets for his gloves. He pulled them on, then leaned forward and kissed her, sweetly, deliberately, lingeringly, and when he drew back, it was all Katherine could do not to follow up that kiss with another.

It was that silly coat, she thought. If he just didn't look so damned attractive in it. "You should button up," she told him. "It's cold outside."

He fumbled with the buttons obediently, but Katherine brushed his hands aside and began the job herself. "You should have put on your gloves after you buttoned your coat," she said as she perfected the first closure and moved down. "It makes this easier, you know."

"This seems pretty easy."

She glanced up to see his smile, lost her momentum, and had to start over with the same button. "I can never get this button to work," she said, feeling a little giddy, a lot nervous. "It always wants to stick."

"You sound like you've done this before."

"Hundreds of times in my fan—" She realized

what she was saying at the same instant he did, and she thought that if ever the time had been right to die of embarrassment, this was it. From the look in his eyes and the charming tug of humor at the corner of his lips, she figured he was piecing together some details of that particular fantasy and decided she could only make things worse by trying to deny it. So she just stepped back and shooed him toward the door. "Just go," she said.

Thankfully, he went.

Chapter Nine

Gabe was back the next afternoon.

"Is it Saturday?" Andy asked excitedly when he opened the door. "Are we going to the North Pole now?"

"Tomorrow, kiddo. Early."

"Hiya, Gabe!" Abby bounced up behind her brother and hopped in place, alternating from one foot to the other. "What's that?" She pointed to the bulge under his coat, and Gabe tried to look as astonished as the juggler had when the monkey crawled out of his shirt, but the twins weren't interested. They just wanted to know what he'd brought them.

"This?" he asked, reaching in to withdraw a fuzzy orange ball. "This is—"

"Matilda!" Abby screeched, reaching for the kitten with both hands. "It's The Real Cat Matilda!"

Katherine was in the room in less than a second, her gray eyes taking in the scene, her face forming the exact expression Gabe had been attempting…a dead ringer for yesterday's juggler.

"Mom…." Abby's voice held all the wonder of

the ages. "Gabe found The Real Cat Matilda and brought her home."

"Hello, Matilda," Andy crooned as he stroked its fuzzy ear. "Hello, kitty."

As both children cuddled around the kitten, Gabe stepped into the apartment and closed the door. He didn't have to try to look sheepish. "Hi, Kate," he began brightly, innocently. "How are you?"

Her frosty look fell to the fuzzball. "Allergic."

"Oh." That put a new perspective on things. "You're allergic to kittens?"

"No, but I'm about to be." She grabbed his arm and tugged him away from the cooing huddle of youngsters. "What are you doing with that cat?"

"You said it would be all right to bring my pet for a visit."

"You said you had a dog. An obedience-trained dog."

"I did," he admitted, wishing that this one time Louisa had done what he asked her to do...which was to find a dog he could borrow for the afternoon...instead of doing what she thought best... which was to spend way too much money to purchase a pedigreed feline because it happened to match the description of Abby's stuffed lion. He hadn't even asked how she knew about the lion. "I did say I had a dog," he continued. "But he was busy this afternoon."

"So you brought your cat instead?"

He loved the flush of irritation on her cheeks, the sparkle of agitation in her eyes. But what he loved most right now was her lips. Her enchanting, kissable lips. "Actually, I brought *your* cat."

"No, you didn't. Tell me you didn't."

"I had to. It came with papers that had to be filled out, and I figured it would be better to put down your name instead of Abby's, and, well, you'll be getting a whole packet of pedigree in the mail in a couple of weeks."

She frowned. A serious frown. A downright murderous frown. "You'll have to take it and its papers back wherever it came from."

Gabe shifted uneasily. Louisa had assured him that Katherine would take one look at the kitten and fall in love. She'd promised. "Now, Kate, I know you said you didn't want a kitten, but you also said you wanted to learn how to purr, and I thought you and Matilda might put your heads together and—"

"Listen to me, Gabe Housley. I am never, ever, going to learn how to purr! Now, you just take that fuzzy little lion back where you found her and maybe, in about twenty years, I'll forget how mad I am at you."

Twenty years. She was still going to be mad about this in twenty years. He wondered if she'd still look this pretty, and if he'd still be so eager to kiss her.

"And you can just wipe that stupid smile off your face, too, because when you leave—in about two minutes from now—the cat goes with you."

"Mom, look." Abby held up the kitten. "She has a spot on her foot, just like the other Matilda. She *is* The Real Cat Matilda. She is!"

"Abby, you know a stuffed toy can't suddenly become real. That spot is just some grape juice you spilled a long time ago."

Abby picked up the kitten's paw and checked the

spot, then hugged the kitten intensely. "I spilled grape juice on you," she murmured in a lullaby. "When you were just a toy."

"For heaven's sake, Abby, you spilled the juice on the stuffed animal, not the cat."

Abby had her hands on warm, fuzzy love, and she wasn't giving in. "That proves she's The Real Cat Matilda! If I hadn't spilt the juice, how could she have this spot in the exact same place?"

"Give the cat back to Gabe, Abby. She doesn't belong to you."

"Yes, she does!" Abby first pulled the cat closer, out of adult reach, hugging it against her heart. Then she abruptly changed tactics and thrust the animal into Katherine's unsuspecting hands. "But she is real, Mom! Feel her! She's the most perfectest Matilda I could ever have."

"Most perfect," Katherine corrected as she awkwardly tried to balance the kitten, which made a soft mewling sound as it huddled, with a delicate shiver, in the palms of her hands. "Most perfect," she repeated, looking down at the kitten's little triangle of a face.

Gabe held his breath and counted all the way to seven before he detected the softening around her eyes. He reached twelve before her expression changed from *Absolutely not!* to *Oh, it's so scared....* The same thing had happened at the office, with Wendy, and with every other female pitted against the kitten's piquant stare.

"Meow?" said The Real Cat Matilda...and the good deed was accomplished.

KATHERINE rolled Abby's parka into a bundle and fitted it under her seat in row 15, orchestra section, Radio City Music Hall. As she straightened, she purposely jostled Gabe's elbow, pushing it from the narrow armrest between their theater seats.

"Let me know if my arm gets in your way," he said, propping his elbow back on the armrest.

She slid an accusing glance at him, empowered by the knowledge that he owed her. He owed her bigtime. And she took serene delight in reminding him at every opportunity. "Your arm is in my way," she said pleasantly.

With a display of deference, he removed his elbow from the armrest, and she contentedly replaced it with hers. Opening the program, she leafed through the pages, just to show how unconcerned she was about his studied regard. "For Pete's sake, Katherine," he said eventually. "You *like* the darn cat."

She shrugged. "Maybe I will learn to like the cat, Gabe, but you needn't think I'm going to forgive you, because I'm not."

"You should be grateful I showed up with the kitten instead of without it."

"Grateful? I should be *grateful?*"

He nodded, crossing his arms across his chest...which, she hadn't been able to help noticing, was nicely covered today by a dark-gold sweater that complemented the rich brown of his eyes. "A less considerate man might have shown up empty-handed and asked you to help him unbutton his coat."

Her cheeks blushed warm—as he'd undoubtedly known they would—and she was grateful the lights had already begun to dim. "A more considerate man wouldn't have shown up," she said, too loudly.

"Sssshhhh, Mom!" Andy leaned around Gabe's far side to reprimand her for continuing to talk in the quieting darkness of the huge auditorium. "The show's getting ready to start."

Gabe arched his eyebrows in a follow-up scold, and on Katherine's other side, Abby flashed her Santa globe flashlight and kicked the seat in front of her. "I still don't see why I couldn't bring Matilda," she muttered. "She likes the Rockettes just as much as me."

Katherine closed the program and, with a glance to make sure Gabe wasn't paying attention, she let her elbow drop from the armrest to a lower, more comfortable position. As the orchestra begin to play and the curtain rose, Abby and Andy sat straight, scooted to the edges of their respective seats and stared at the stage, their jaws slack, their mouths rounded in fascinated and duplicate *O*s.

Gabe leaned close to Katherine, bringing with him a sensual and subtle awareness. "Keep your eyes open for Santa Claus," he whispered. "If he's here, I don't want you to blink and miss seeing him."

She sighed at his teasing, thinking how good he smelled, how solid his shoulder was when she occasionally brushed against it. It was a wondrously strange feeling to be sitting next to him in the dark, surrounded on every side, but very much alone together.

She usually sat through the Christmas Spectacular with just the twins, although some years, she invited friends to join them. Despite the emphasis on Santa

Claus, she couldn't deny the magical quality of hearing the ageless melodies of Christmas performed in this huge old charmer of a theater. She had been busy and failed to get tickets this year, had even been thinking they'd skip seeing the Rockettes this one time, but when Gabe produced four tickets for this afternoon's show, she'd been as excited as the kids. And when she met his eyes over their bobbing red heads, it had been as if she were making an assignation with her lover.

So now, here she was, ensconced between her twins like always, but with Gabe ensconced there with her. She had said she wanted him to go away and stay away, but in every way that counted, she had invited him to stay. So why was she surprised to find him beside her, making the three of them an even four? Was it possible that she, like Abby, had willed her harmless stuffed lion into a living, breathing reality? Had Gabe, like The Real Cat Matilda, become something more than a fantasy because her heart wanted so badly for him to be real?

Katherine closed her eyes, then opened them again, getting her focus straight. There was no truth to be found in fantasy. It wasn't real. It wasn't meant to be. Being intangible was its charm, its attraction, and its only reality.

Onstage, a little boy began singing "I Saw Mommy Kissing Santa Claus," and in the darkness, Gabe took her hand and held it as if he never meant to let go.

"I LIKED the Sugarbear Fairies the best!" Abby announced happily as she hopped out of the taxi, still talking about the show they'd seen well over two hours ago. Gabe was beginning to wonder when she'd ever stop talking about it. "But you know what, Gabe?"

He handed the driver a bill to cover the fare and waved away the change, then caught hold of the pink parka hood. "What, Abby?"

"I liked the ice-skaters the best of all!"

"I remember you said that." At least a hundred times, if his excellent memory served.

"I liked the camels. Those were *real* camels, weren't they, Gabe?" Andy cleared the cab in a two-fisted jump onto the curb. "And *real* sheeps and a *real* donkey!"

"Sheep." Katherine climbed out after him, accepting the brief assistance of Gabe's gloved hand, reaching protectively for Andy almost in the same instant. Gabe caught her gaze and held it for a moment in which every impatient thought that had flitted through his brain in the past hours vanished into the sweetness of her appreciative smile. For no good reason he could name, he felt as if he'd saved her from a burning building. If he thought it would result in another smile like that one, he'd gladly sit through the Rockettes' show every day for a month. Well, maybe not *gladly*, but he'd do it.

Abby began to tug on his hand. "Come on, Gabe, let's go check on The Real Cat Matilda."

Andy whirled out of Katherine's grasp and into Gabe's as the four of them skirted the pedestrian traffic to reach the front door of the co-op. "Are you cooking dinner for us tonight, too, Gabe?"

"Didn't we just eat dinner at that weird restaurant you recommended?"

"Oh, yeah. Jekyll and Hyde." Andy's memory caught up to his overstimulated enthusiasm. "I didn't forget. I was just trickin' ya. Jekyll and Hyde was way cool. I can't wait to tell Tyler I got to go there. Didn't I tell ya it was a cool place?"

"I remember you said that." He smiled at Raymond, who was holding the door for them. "Evening, Raymond."

"Got a delivery for you," Raymond said. "Arrived just after you'd left for the show this afternoon."

"A delivery?" Gabe guided first one twin, then the other, through the doorway after Katherine. "Why would I get a delivery here?"

"Louisa brought it by." Raymond walked around them and stepped behind the doorman's station. He bent down, then straightened again as he passed a narrow leather strap around the counter. "Congratulations—it's a Schnauzer. His name's Champion Crystal Blue Persuasion, and Louisa says he's yours on approval until Tuesday."

Gabe followed the leash until he was face to bearded muzzle with a hefty salt-and-pepper dog of medium height, who was sitting obediently behind the station, his ears pointed, his bushy eyebrows angled over dark, intelligent eyes. "Hello." Gabe scratched the ears, and the eyes drooped in ecstasy. "Now, what does Louisa think I'm going to do with you?"

"Whatta ya got?" Andy barrelled up behind him

and bumped against his shoulder. "It's a dog," the boy whispered in awe. "It's a *real* dog."

Braids bouncing, Abby came over to investigate. "A dog," she said happily. "Does he belong to us?"

"I guess he does...at least until Tuesday."

"Us?" Katherine's voice came over the desk, all but thumping him between the shoulder blades. "Oh, no. He may belong to you, Gabe, but he definitely does *not* belong to us."

"Well, he doesn't belong here with me, that's for sure." Raymond pulled a duffel bag out from under the credenza and hefted it into Gabe's arms. "This belongs to the champ, here. Food, vitamins, shampoo, clothes, the works. Louisa said it was all in there, even a toothbrush."

"Clothes?" Abby echoed with interest. "A toothbrush?"

"Hello," Andy crooned, as he knelt in front of the dog. "Hello, doggy."

Katherine leaned further over the counter. "He comes with his own toothbrush?"

"What's his name?" Andy patted the dog with both hands and then kissed him on the mouth.

"Andy, don't kiss the—" Katherine began.

"His name?" Gabe repeated, his gaze intercepting Katherine's protest and diverting it to him in a look of wary comprehension. "His name is Crystal Blue Persuasion, but since crystal is glass and glass sparkles, well...for short, we just call him—"

"Sparky!" Andy supplied, throwing his arms around the schnauzer's neck.

Gabe felt like the man of the hour as he watched the bonding of boy and dog. The feeling dwindled to man of the minute, however, when he met Katherine's furious gaze. He offered his best what-else-could-I-say? shrug, and received her reply in an I'll-murder-you-for-this glare. Maybe, he thought, it would have been better to call the dog Champ.

EVERY LIGHT in the house was on when Gabe walked in. He found Gun in the kitchen, making a salad. "Hello, Junior. Want something to eat?"

"No, thanks." Gabe turned one of the ladder-back chairs around and straddled it. "I ate at a restaurant where the main source of ambience comes from trying to scare the stuffing out of the customers."

"Not your usual choice of eatery," Gun commented.

"It came highly recommended," he said wryly.

Gun chopped some cauliflower and tossed it in the bowl. "You're home kinda early."

"Have to get an early start tomorrow." Gabe feigned interest in the salad bowl, avoiding the real reason he was home, doing his best to block out the memory of Katherine's don't-let-the-door-hit-you-in-the-butt goodbye. "If Louisa found a pilot willing to fly to the North Pole, that is."

"What do you mean, *if?*" Gun leveled a slice of red pepper at Gabe. "If that woman can find a furball in Tiffany's and a canine in Cartier's, she can damn well find a pilot."

"I wondered where she had to go to find such expensive animals." Gabe set his chin on his hands and watched Gun peel a tomato. "I guess you know all about the cat, the dog, and how mad Katherine is."

"Don't look so glum," Gun advised. "It's Christmas. Seeing Santa's workshop tomorrow will perk her right up. Parents always enjoy seeing their kids have fun."

"I'm counting on that, but I'm beginning to think it would have been a whole lot easier to have just asked her out to dinner and a show."

"So why haven't you?" Gun asked. "Not that it's any of my business, of course, but who are you courting? Her or her kids?"

"She's a package deal, Dad. A three-in-one special." Gabe offered the theory he'd formulated during his walk home. "I can't decide whether she's protecting the twins or herself, but there are moments—a lot of them—when I'm afraid Abby and Andy are the only reason I get to spend any time with her, at all."

"And you want to spend time with her?"

"Oh, yeah," Gabe said, positive of that, if nothing else. "I've only known her a couple of days, but somehow, I believe I could spend the rest of my life just watching her move. I think I could get lost for weeks in her smile. And when she laughs..." He broke off self-consciously. "Well, you get the picture."

"No wonder she's not so anxious to be alone with you. If I thought you felt that way about me, I'd be scared to death."

"You can relax, because I *don't* feel that way about you. But I do feel that way about Katherine. It scares me out of my wits, but from the moment I looked up and saw her standing in my office doorway, I've felt as though I were hurtling toward her like some out-of-control comet.''

Gun put down his knife and looked Gabe straight in the eyes. "I knew two minutes after I met your mother, God rest her soul, that she was the only woman I would ever want to wake up to. I might have known sooner, but I was wearing sunglasses the first time I saw her." He leaned forward, assuming his good-advice posture. "I'm going to break my standing rule of parenting, Junior, and give you some good advice. There's not a woman out there who wants to be a three-for-one deal, no matter what she says. Make up your mind what it is you're attracted to, because unless it's just her—the very essence of who she is—then you should walk away now, and I mean this minute."

Gabe frowned, then pushed up from the chair and scooted it under the table. "I was sort of hoping you'd tell me that if I took a couple of aspirin and went to bed, I wouldn't feel like a comet in the morning."

Gun picked up his knife. "Always happy to cement the father-son bond by telling you things you don't want to know. Speaking of not wanting to know, what did you do with the animals?"

"Left them with the kids, of course. She's mad, but she's not crazy. The combined forces of the police and fire departments couldn't have pried one furry paw out of that apartment tonight."

Gun whittled a carrot into a dozen slivers. "You should have cleared it with her before you went giving pets to the kids."

"I didn't originally intend to *give* them the pets. I

just thought the twins would play with them for a while and then I'd send the animals back.''

Gun popped the remaining matchstick of carrot into his mouth and chewed, giving Gabe one of his I-raised-a-moron looks. "These kids have got your number, Junior. I'm telling you, you better be real sure you want the whole package before you go getting involved with this woman.''

"You just told me not to think of her as a package, Dad.''

"Well, what do I know? When I met your mother, you weren't part of the deal.''

"Would it have made a difference to you, if I had been?''

"Nope. You might have made things a little inconvenient, but it wouldn't have made any difference. Your mother could have come with a dozen kids and it wouldn't have made a string bean's worth of difference to me.''

"A dozen kids would have been damned inconvenient, though, wouldn't they, Dad?''

Gun grinned as he reached for a stalk of celery. "Well, you know how I love a challenge. Next time, though, ask the mother before you go giving the kids presents. It'll make your life a lot simpler.''

"I certainly wish you'd told me that this morning.''

"How was I to know you'd pull such a harebrained stunt?''

"You seem to know everything else.''

"Not before it happens, I don't." Gun tossed in the chopped celery. "I sure as heck don't know what you're going to do with a dog and cat while we're gone tomorrow.''

''We?''

''You asked Louisa to find a pilot, and she got you the best. But I warn you, I don't work cheap.''

Gabe was pleased, despite his best efforts not to show it. ''Are you sure you can fit a trip to the North Pole in between stakeouts?''

''McClellan's been calling the office again. This way it'll be the truth when you tell him I've been out of the city. He doesn't need to know it was only for the weekend.''

Gabe walked to the doorway and paused. ''Do you think Louisa would keep the animals while we're gone?''

Gun was still laughing when Gabe reached the stairs and headed up to bed.

KATHERINE AWOKE the next morning with a warm, fuzzy feeling. Two of them, to be exact. One at her feet and one at her neck. From the snuffling intermittent snores rising from the foot of the bed and the steady purring hum near her ear, she named the feelings Sparky and The Real Cat Matilda, come to join her slumbers sometime during the night. Being well acquainted with the rambunctious sleep patterns of her children, she couldn't blame the animals. On the occasions when the twins crept into her bed in the night, she was forced to creep out and catch the sandman as best she could on the sofa. She moved her foot beneath the sheet and the sounds of sleep stopped, as each of the warm spots beside her stirred, sensing, perhaps, that she was awake and that it was their role as companions to join her in that state, as well.

Yawning, Katherine looked at the ceiling and thought how nice it would be to snooze for another half hour...except that there was a copious energy tickling her foggy, precaffeine brain. *Get up,* it said. *Gabe will be here soon. Get up. Get up. Get up.*

The North Pole, she thought. She was going to the North Pole. How had Gabe come up with such a ridiculous destination? Not that she believed for a second that he meant to fly them all to the northern-most tip of the earth. She had intended to talk to Abby and Andy about that very thing last night. But the dog had had to be walked and the cat had had to be tended, and the twins had been just like any other child with a new pet...too excited to talk about any-thing else. When they bounded out of bed this morn-ing—which probably would happen any minute now—it would be pointless to try to tell them that today's trip basically involved a town that merely capitalized on its name and the Santa mythology.

At this point, she doubted anything she said would make any difference. They'd had more excitement in the past couple of days than in their entire first seven years, and probably more than they'd have in the next seven. Gabe was throwing pleasure at them as if it were confetti, and they were grabbing greedy handfuls of it.

Well, he'd created their ridiculously high expec-tations, and when the disappointment came, whatever it turned out to be, he'd just have to deal with it.

Right, she thought as the kitten nuzzled her ear. As if he'd dealt with the aftermath of a single issue so far. For a while after he left last night, she'd considered the possibility that he was skipping the drink-dinner-theater seduction scene and taking the see-how-great-I-am-with-kids approach to her bedroom. She knew women who fell for that, had even dated one man who tried it. The jerk had come right out and told her he wouldn't have been so nice to her kids if he knew she wasn't going to show her appreciation.

But if that had been Gabe's idea to begin with, he was certainly going overboard with it. He came, he saw, he provided. If Andy had an imaginary dog, then Gabe would make it real. If Abby believed her stuffed lion was a kitten in disguise, so it was. If the twins wanted to find Santa Claus, then Gabe would find him and, if a satisfactory Santa couldn't be found in New York City, then there was nothing for it but to fly Abby and Andy to the North Pole and look for him there. Katherine was beginning to think that if the twins expressed a desire to visit the man in the moon, Gabe would pick up the phone and call NASA.

She worried that this wasn't good for them. She knew it wasn't good for her. What was more seductive than a man who was the spitting image of her bedroom fantasies and who, in addition, just happened to be crazy about her kids? But how could she trust him with their hearts, as well as hers? Maybe if she and Gabe had dated first, before this crazy Santa search began, she wouldn't feel so threatened. But he had stepped right out of her fantasies into Abby's and Andy's reality, and she didn't know how to stop the momentum of his mad plunge into her life and the lives of her children. She didn't know enough about the laws of physics to stick out a metaphorical foot and trip him. And the truth was, she wanted him to be real.

Katherine sighed and stretched, dislodging the kitten, who roused and began exercising its claws in a pleasant, scratchy massage of her shoulder. Really, it was amazing how much the kitten looked like Abby's stuffed lion. And that spot on her paw...well, it did look a little like a grape-juice stain.

Sparky shook himself, the tags on his collar tinkling like an alarm clock. He looked at her expectantly and, God help her, she laughed. There, in her bed, with a dog she was going to have to take outside for a walk, and a kitten she was beginning to imagine was a toy come to life, she laughed. Gabe had a lot to answer for. But she was going to spend the day with him on a North Pole trip she never would have planned herself, with children whose eyes lately held a happiness she hadn't known they'd missed. Much as she wanted to deny it, she knew that Gabe—in his well-meaning, mule-headed manner—had made her world a better place to wake up in.

Now, if only she could keep her world safe...keep herself from falling in love with him, one heart at a time.

Chapter Ten

For a small plane, the Cessna wasn't nerve-jangling noisy. At least, it hadn't been before Andy and Abby got in it. Gun had obtained fifteen minutes of wide-eyed quiet by instructing them to listen for big bangs, rattles, or the sound of something falling off during take-off. But once they were airborne, all bets were off.

"Will all the reindeer be there?"

"Do you think we might see a polar bear?"

"I want to see a walrus."

"Santa doesn't have a walrus, dummy."

"He could have one if he wanted. Santa could have a walrus, couldn't he, Gabe?"

"When will we get there? I see something red. I bet that's Rudolph's nose! Is that his nose, Gabe?"

"I can see Santa's whole workshop from my window."

"No, you can't. You're just saying that 'cause you can't see Rudolph's nose."

"I can too see it. I can see everything from my window. All the reindeer and everything. Can't I, Gabe?"

From her position in the copilot's seat, Katherine looked over her shoulder and smiled serenely at the magpies. From his position in the center of the bench seat and between the magpies, Gabe noticed that she didn't include him in that affectionate look. When her gaze did settle on his for a moment, he offered her his brightest boy-am-I-having-fun grin. She touched her ear, indicating that she couldn't hear— although he hadn't tried to say anything to her. Then she turned around and said something to Gun, who laughed and made a comment that in turn caused her to laugh and say something else in response.

In the back seat, Gabe told himself he couldn't be—was *not,* in fact—jealous because Gun was enjoying a conversation with Katherine while he, Gabe, was playing satellite dish to the twins' transmission of jabber. No, indeed, he was not feeling impatient or frustrated or any other remotely negative emotion. He'd planned this trip for the twins' enjoyment and he'd be positive if it killed him…or left him deaf, which seemed much more likely at the moment.

He was enjoying this time with the twins, really he was. It wasn't their fault that, upon arriving at their apartment to pick them up, he had been unprepared for the logical seven-year-old assumption that the dog and the kitten would be accompanying them on the trip. And, as Katherine had pointed out, it wasn't her place to tell them. He probably should have realized they'd be upset when he explained that the animals couldn't come, that they would, in fact, have to stay in a kennel over the weekend. He couldn't have known that kids took forever to say goodbye to their pets, but if he *had* known, he would have started out earlier. Then they wouldn't have been late in getting to the airport, Gun wouldn't have hustled them into the plane, and Gabe might have had a reasonable chance of getting the seating arrangements he'd had in mind...namely, separating the twins, instead of him and Katherine.

But he wasn't worried. Once they arrived at the amusement park, everything would go just as he'd planned. The twins would gambol through the Christmas village, enjoying themselves, while he and Katherine strolled along, holding hands and discovering the delights to be found in just staring into each other's eyes. And at the end of the day, she'd thank him for showing her that magic did exist in the world, that there was room in her heart for Santa Claus, that there was room in her life for him, her hero.

Okay, so maybe he'd had one too many cups of cocoa when he imagined the joyous possibilities of the day. But just being with Katherine was good. Just watching her laugh was a fine thing. Even if it was Gun who was both instigator and beneficiary of that laughter. Even if Gabe's own ears were ringing from all the childhood joy on either side of him.

"I can see Dancer and Prancer and Donover and Blizzard and... What's the reindeer's name that comes after Blizzard, Gabe?"

Despite his excellent memory, Jackass was the only name that sprang to mind.

GUN MONOPOLIZED Katherine's attention the rest of the day. While Gabe chased two energetic redheads he hadn't a prayer of catching, his father and the redheads' mother talked, laughed, and had a wonderful time...the wonderful time he, in fact, had planned to have himself.

But Andy and Abby had other ideas for him. He'd brought them to the North Pole and Santa's workshop and they wanted him to see every Christmasy inch of it with them. When he suggested that, of course, they'd want their mother to see it, too, they reminded him *she* had taken one look at the authentic one-and-only North Pole Santa's workshop Santa Claus and remarked, "Nice suit. Wonder where he rented it." Oh, no, the twins assured Gabe. *She* would only keep *them* from having fun.

So while Gabe was dragged, like a dog on a leash, from Santa's house to the Jack Jingle Theater to the reindeer corral to the post office to the World of Christmas Gift Shop and through every other imaginable place Abby or Andy could think to go in and out of, Gun and Katherine lingered in the warmth of Mother Hubbard's Kitchen, enjoying a cup of coffee and each other's conversation. While Gabe pretended to know elf names and reindeer games, he imagined Gun spinning his wildly romantic and greatly exaggerated tales of life as a private investigator. And it didn't help that every time he saw Katherine, she was either smiling, laughing or listening intently in response to whatever Gun was saying.

But then, suddenly, things began to look up. When one of Santa's denim-clad helpers—not an elf, because, as Andy had previously reminded Gabe, elves wore green—announced it was time for "elfin training" and took responsibility for herding the twins into Santa's house, Gabe saw his opportunity. The air was getting colder, the sky grayer, when he finally located Katherine, sitting alone and sipping coffee in the Jack Spratt Bake Shop. "Hi," he said. "The twins are learning to be elves. I hope that's okay."

"As long as they're not learning to be imps, I think we're safe." Her smile made him thank whatever kind Fates had decreed the sweet curve of her mouth. "Gun went to check on the weather. He said he didn't like the looks of that sky."

Gabe waved away any threat. "Tonight's the tree-trimming party. A little snow isn't going to stop that."

"Andy and Abby are really looking forward to making paper chains and decorating a real tree. They're having a wonderful time here, Gabe."

He started to ask her how she knew, since she had barely seen them in the past couple of hours, but she was smiling still, and he didn't want to ruin it. "I'm sorry you're stuck with Dad. If I'd known he wouldn't entertain himself, I wouldn't have invited him to come along." Under the circumstances, Gabe decided, he could stretch the truth a little. "He says he's lonely, and I felt sorry for him. But if I'd had any idea he was going to bore you to flinders, well, I'd have left him home with a clear conscience."

Katherine took a sip of coffee and Gabe watched the parting of her lips with something akin to envy for the coffee cup. "That's funny," she said. "Gun said if it wasn't for him agreeing at the last minute to be the pilot, you'd have had to cancel the trip."

Gabe sighed, wondering if he could retroactively put Gun in the rest home for aging detectives. "He probably followed up that comment by telling you I have a perfectly valid private pilot's license, which has never done anything except gather dust in the bottom of my sock drawer.''

"Actually, he said you keep it tucked in with your underwear.''

Gabe dropped his head on his arms, but when he heard her soft laughter, he straightened.

"What he told me, Gabe, was that you got the license because you wanted to prove you could, but decided afterwards that you didn't like flying and put it away.''

"I don't mind flying solo so much," Gabe explained, at the insistence of his ego. "I just have a little problem piloting other people. Being responsible for someone else is a lot different than just taking responsibility for me.''

"Really?" she agreed with a wry smile. "He said that about you, too.''

"What? That I can't handle responsibility?''

"No, he said you take it very seriously.''

"Oh." Gabe studied her thoughtfully. "What else has he been telling you about me?''

"Do you want the unabridged list, or just the highlights?''

Gabe was immediately ashamed of himself for feeling even a moment's jealousy of the time his dad had spent with Katherine. Gun had obviously spent the time talking about what a great guy his son was. Following quickly on that thought was the realization of all the embarrassing details Gun could have—and probably had—told this woman. "Please tell me he didn't share the rosebud story," Gabe asked, without any real hope.

"I thought that one was very romantic. No one's ever risked hard labor just to spell out my name in rosebuds. I hope little Rosalinda was appropriately impressed."

"She stayed home from school that day and never even saw my masterpiece. I spent two years working after school and Saturdays to pay back the florist for the roses I beheaded. He was more than repaid, believe me."

"Gun said he thought it an excellent lesson for you in the perils of thievery."

"Well, I still stand by my original reasoning that if they grow back, it isn't stealing." He cupped his hands around hers, there on Jack Spratt's table, and leaned forward. "I'm sorry you've had to listen to Dad's assorted stories of my illustrious childhood. I'll make it up to you, somehow."

"Please don't apologize. You don't know how happy I am to have the means to blackmail you."

Gabe tried to look as dismayed as possible while holding her hand. "You wouldn't."

"Oh, yes, I would. I'm already looking forward to it with unflattering *relish.*"

He closed his eyes. "He surely didn't tell you about the relish trays."

She nodded. "Right down to the centerpiece tub of 'passion dip' and the assorted multicolored 'condom-ments.' I think if you'd been a little older, he would have encouraged you to market the idea, instead of just giving them as gifts to your friends."

"Male friends," Gabe qualified. "And that was only in my young-guy stage of development. I have matured."

"I know. He told me about the stripper at your last birthday party, too."

"That party was five years ago," Gabe said in hurried self-defense. "And it was right after my divorce, and—" He stopped. "I suppose you're fully informed on the details of that, too?"

Katherine finally looked a little less amused than before. "He just said you married someone you'd dated for years and that you had a reasonably amicable divorce six months after the ceremony."

"Well, at least he didn't outline the terms of the settlement...did he?"

She shook her head, her hair swinging forward to brush her cheeks. "He skipped that and went straight to the birthday party."

"Well, no matter what he said, my role in the stripper incident was greatly exaggerated. She was obviously nervous, and I thought if I took off my shirt, she'd feel more comfortable, and things got a little out of hand and—" Realizing this story wasn't going to enhance her opinion of him, Gabe changed the subject in midsentence. "I wanted to spend more time with you on this trip," he said. "Maybe tonight, after the tree-trimming, we can...you and I can take a walk...or something."

"I vote for the 'or something.'"

He looked into her eyes and decided this trip was going *so* much better than he'd planned.

Then Gun stomped in to tell them the cold front had dipped farther south than predicted and they had somewhere in the neighborhood of two hours to fly out or get stranded in the blizzard sweeping toward the North Pole.

"IT'S NOT SNOWING." Abby pressed her face to the window of the cab. "See? There's not a blizzard."

"There hasn't been one itsy, bitsy snowflake since we left Santa's workshop." Andy hunkered down next to Katherine, his arms crossed, his lower lip extended in a full pout, his narrowed gaze searing a hole in the back of Gabe's neck.

Gabe was tired. He was tired of being patient. He was tired of traveling. He was tired of sitting in a seat that was either behind or in front of the one in which Katherine was sitting. But most of all, he was tired of explaining to two overstimulated, whiny and disappointed seven-year-olds that just because it was not snowing where they were now, that didn't mean there wasn't a blizzard where they had been earlier.

"You promised, Gabe." Abby flounced away from the window and leaned forward so that he could hear her. "You promised we'd see Rudolph."

"I wanted to see Rudolph." Andy tossed his petulant complaint toward Gabe's other ear. "And the *real* Santa. You said the real Santa would be there and he wasn't. It was just another guy in a red suit."

"Andy," Katherine murmured quietly. "Let's not talk about this anymore."

"But I'm mad, Mom. Gabe said we'd find Santa Claus and he said we'd get to go out and cut down a real tree and he said we'd get to make paper chains and stuff to put on it and now we don't get to and it's not even snowing!"

"I know," Katherine said patiently.

"Yeah." Abby slumped back to join in the airing of grievances. "Gabe made us leave Santa's house before we ever even learnt how to be elves!"

"Learned," Katherine said, her tone still soft and soothing. "That one elf... What was her name?"

"Dopey," Andy muttered, and Katherine hurried on with her attempt to comfort.

"Well, whatever her name is, she gave you each a Santa hat to bring home, didn't she? That was nice."

"No, it wasn't, Mom. Her name was Kerri and she wasn't a real elf. She was just a helper. Besides, Gabe already bought us Santa hats in the gift shop."

"Well, then you have two apiece, don't you?" There was an edge of impatience in her tone that time. Just an edge, but somehow it made Gabe feel a little better. He thought he'd feel a whole lot better if she'd just tell them to shut up and be done with it. He knew she wouldn't, knew he didn't really want her to. He even knew that if she did, he'd have an immediate paradigm shift and feel sympathetic toward the kids and irritated with her. They were children. They were disappointed. And in their minds, it had to be someone's fault.

So, okay, Gabe would be the fall guy. He'd listen to their whiny voices and bear the indignity of having saved them from spending Christmas in a hotel room. Even if the blizzard turned out to be just another heavy snow in the Adirondacks, the decision to leave when they had had been the right one. Even if Abby and Andy were mad at him. Even if they didn't believe him about the snow.

"I wanted to be an elf."

"I wanted to see Rudolph."

Gabe just wanted to go home. He thought wistfully of Gun, who'd taken another cab. Katherine had urged him to go with his dad, told him she and the twins didn't need an escort to their door. But he couldn't do that. He'd set up their expectations, and it wasn't fair to ask Katherine to bear the brunt of their disappointment. He'd see them home and into bed. Then he'd kiss Katherine good-night and head home to bed himself. And tomorrow, all would be forgiven. All would be well. Tomorrow, they'd like him and he'd like them again.

"Gabe promised, Mom," Andy said. "He promised we'd find Santa Claus at the North Pole."

Katherine tried to hold on to her patience, but it was getting harder by the minute. She was sorry she'd ever agreed to this trip. But then, she hadn't agreed, had she? Gabe had just pushed his plan on her, the same way he'd pushed this whole stupid Santa search, the same way he'd pushed the dog and cat into her life. "There was a very nice man playing Santa Claus, Andy," she said, revealing none of her exasperation. "He even had a real beard."

"But he had bad breath, Mom. He smelled like fish guts."

"*Andy!* I don't want to hear anything more about this. You knew better than to believe you were going to find the real Santa Claus at the North Pole...or anywhere else you've looked. It's not fair to blame Gabe because you wanted to believe something that isn't true, now is it?"

"No, Mom."

Katherine looked at Abby with the same question.

"Gabe shouldn't have told us there was a Santa Claus when there wasn't," Abby concluded. "And he shouldn't have said there was a blizzard when it wasn't even snowing. He shouldn't have done that."

"I think it was very nice of him to want to take you in an airplane to a place you've never been, just because he thought you'd have a good time. And you *did* have a good time. It isn't Gabe's fault the weather turned bad."

"But, Mom, it isn't snowing!" Andy scooted restlessly on the seat. "We could've stayed and decorated the tree and had all the things in Abby's picture just like Gabe said we would and now we can't and it's not *fair!*"

"What picture?" Katherine asked, not sure whether this was an imagined part of the day's disappointments, or something else.

"The picture Abby drew of what we want for Christmas. We gave it to Gabe with five dollars and he said he'd get it for us."

Katherine caught the look of protest Gabe tossed toward the back seat of the cab, but he didn't utter a word of denial. "What was in the picture?" she asked.

"Nothing," Andy said morosely. "It was just a dumb old picture."

"It wasn't neither dumb." Abby made a face at her brother in defense of her art. "It was a picture of our family, Mom. Me and Andy and you and Sparky, and The Real Cat Matilda, and a house, and a Christmas tree, and cookies we made and stockings we hung on the fireplace and a whole week with our daddy."

The last was slipped in innocently, but Katherine not only caught her son's quick, cautious glance and her daughter's accusing glare at the man sitting in front of her, she saw the stiffening of Gabe's shoulders and knew the truth of the matter. Gabe had set her children up for a disappointment much greater than she'd anticipated.

Promising to deliver Santa Claus was one thing. Katherine hadn't liked the idea, but she'd been teaching Abby and Andy the difference between fantasy and reality since they were old enough to talk. She knew they had enough grasp of the truth to counteract whatever nonsense they heard about a silly fat man in a red suit. Until just now, she'd felt reasonably secure, if not enthusiastic, about letting them have fun with the idea of looking for Santa Claus, discovering for themselves the truth of what she'd told them. But suddenly she saw the whole "adventure" from a new and dangerous angle.

A picture-perfect Christmas was logical at seven, and it was just as easy to add a "daddy" to the picture as to leave him out. But once he was crayoned in, added like a place setting at the family table, he couldn't be taken out. There would always be that empty place, the reminder of something broken or lost and forever after missing from the table. Gabe might not have—probably had not, in fact—spoken the words, but his actions had fed her children's belief that he could be the daddy they wanted.

And she was guilty, too. Guilty of wanting something more than her original bargain. She'd promised her children before their birth that no father would have any claim on them, that he would not exist as a presence in their lives and would therefore never have the power to betray them. Not as her father had betrayed her.

Until Gabe, until that kiss under the mistletoe last Christmas, it had been an easy promise to keep. But since then, she'd been guilty of imagining her life with him, imagining she could share herself, her life, her children. So, yes, she was guilty, too. Guilty of letting the twins watch as she fell into the trap of believing in something—and someone—who was too good to be true.

But tonight would be the end of it. For her children's sake...and her own...tonight would be the end.

As GOODBYES GO, it went well. A bit stilted, maybe, but that was normal, Katherine thought. Considering that she'd come very close to suggesting Gabe meet her for lunch sometime. But there was no doubt in her mind that lunch would lead to a lunchtime affair, which would lead to dinner, which would lead to weekends, which would involve the twins, which would lead to complications just like this one. It had to be over. Severed cleanly and neatly. No matter how much she might regret losing the only fantasy she'd ever really loved.

For his part, Gabe said very little, listening to her efficient explanation with the same patience he'd exercised on the trip home. He pretended to believe the rationale she presented was as flawless, as impenetrable, as she obviously believed it to be. Tomorrow, he'd decide how to reassure her, how to make her understand that he would never hurt her, that he had no intention of allowing anything that happened between them to affect Abby or Andy. He wanted to tell her that he was just as scared as she was, that the thought of making a commitment to the three-in-one package that was her terrified him. The thing was, he was more terrified of not making it.

But tonight was not the right moment to tell her he loved her. It was not the right moment to say anything except a reluctant and weary good-night.

"I'll bring Sparky and Matilda home on Monday," he said at the door, making it seem casual and normal, as if Katherine hadn't just outlined all the reasons he should never come back again. "And I'll find a pet-care service for you, too."

"That isn't necessary, Gabe."

"It's the least I can do."

"You misunderstood me. I don't want you to bring the pets back on Monday or any other day. I don't want them here at all."

That took him by surprise. "But what about the kids? They'll be heartbroken."

"The animals were only here for a day. If they'd been here when we got back tonight, it would have been harder, but they weren't here. And in a few days, Andy and Abby will forget that the pets were supposed to come back. They may ask about them, may cry a few tears, but Christmas is in a few more days and they'll have new toys to play with and school will start again, and by then, they'll barely remember the dog and cat were ever real at all."

"Do you think you can make them believe they just imagined me, too?"

She didn't want to answer that—he could tell by the way she lowered her eyelashes and looked anywhere except at his face. "You haven't been in their lives long enough to make a dent, Gabe. I'm sorry if that seems unfeeling, but children are very resilient. They forget easily, and Abby and Andy *will* forget you."

The patience he'd clung to vanished, turning to a slow, cold and empty anger. "They might," he said. "But you won't. You won't ever forget, Kate."

Then he kissed her to make sure of it.

THE KISS seared her lips with yearning and burned a fiery memory into her soul, and Katherine's knees went weak with the wanting. She was a fool to be here, to let her arms creep around his neck, to lean into him and align her body along the warm, solid length of his. It was crazy to stand in the open doorway of her apartment, clinging to Gabe as if she couldn't bear to let him go, when it was she who was demanding he leave.

She would ask him to stay, she decided. She'd sneak him into her bedroom and close the door and satisfy this fantasy once and for all. She would undress him, take off his coat one button at a time, remove the rest of his clothes in a fever heat, and finally have her way with him. Not once. Not twice. But all night long. *I want you,* she would tell him. *I want you now...and later...and for the rest of my...*

Her heart stopped beating with the thought, then jerked into a fast and painful rhythm. His hands moved to her hips, pulled her close, held her against him. His body spoke to hers in a thousand languages, all of them silently persuading her that she was a fool if she let him go. Maybe, she thought. Maybe there was a way. It was Christmas, after all. Couldn't she have one gift she didn't have to buy for herself? Couldn't she open one package and be surprised to find what was inside? Gabe could be that gift. He could be the gift she couldn't buy, the surprise she hadn't expected to find. If she could just have Gabe for Christmas, she wouldn't wish for anything else ever again. Just him. Just his kiss. Just this little bit of reality. Just this one Christmas...

But then he put his hands at her waist and set her away from him. "And what about that, Kate? In a few days, are you going to be telling yourself that was a figment of your imagination? Do you still believe this relationship has nowhere to go?"

She swallowed hard and forced her hands to stay at her sides. "I believe, possibly...under different circumstances, maybe...we might have had a really wonderful affair."

His lips tightened, and an aching sadness filtered through the passion that still burned in his eyes. Or maybe, Katherine thought as his hand came up to stroke her face, the aching sadness was all her own. "I guess that's the real difference between us, isn't it, Kate? You want to believe we might have had a wonderful affair. And no matter what the circumstances, I want to believe we might have had a wonderful life."

Then he was gone, striding away from her, down the hallway to the elevators, walking out of her life as quickly and effortlessly as he'd walked in. She closed the door and leaned against it, telling herself she was right. She had to be right. She was sure that sometime tomorrow she'd remember exactly why it had seemed so important to be right. But for tonight, being right meant she was going to bed alone...without Sparky the dog, or The Real Cat Matilda, or even so much as a single, simple Armani coat fantasy to keep her warm.

Chapter Eleven

For the second night in a row, Gabe walked home from Katherine's apartment and found Gun in the kitchen. For the first time since he was a boy, he found him baking cookies. "Thought I'd mix up some gingerbread dough," Gun explained, without having been asked. "Remember how you and I used to make those gingerbread men and hang them on the Christmas tree? Well, I thought you could bring Katherine and the twins over tomorrow afternoon, so we could decorate the tree." Gun glanced up long enough to wink before he returned to his stirring. "Give you and Katherine a little time under the mistletoe...if you know what I mean."

Gabe didn't pull out a chair tonight, didn't feel much like standing, either, but couldn't seem to move on upstairs to bed. "Aren't you tired?" he asked finally, amazed, as always, by his father's seemingly limitless stamina.

"Me? Nah." Gun kneaded the dough with his fingers, squishing it between his knuckles like a kid. "I had a great time today. What's wrong with you? Too much responsibility today for your normally su. spirits?''

"Two too much.'' Gabe moved to the sink and filled a glass with water, which he downed in one long swallow. "Katherine and her children.''

"That adds up to three.''

"No, that adds up to one. One family of three. And one single guy, who from now on is going to mind his own business.''

Gun scraped the cookie dough from his fingers and then wiped them clean with a kitchen towel. "I put that package from the gift shop on your bed. Figured it was my Christmas present, but I'll tell you right now, if it's one of those silly Santa Claus hats, you have some more shopping to do.''

"That's for Katherine.'' Gabe felt like an idiot, just remembering the silly little thing he'd impulsively picked up on one of the twins' forays through the gift shop.

"I don't think she'll want a Santa hat, either.''

"Give me some credit, Dad. It's a ceramic angel. This silly little thing with a starry halo, reaching for a star. A stupid little nothing of a gift. I don't even know why I picked it up.''

"Must have called your name,'' Gun said, paying more attention to his kneading than to the conversation.

"I foolishly imagined it was calling hers.'' Gabe said it under his breath as he set the glass on the countertop with a clatter, wondering if there was any way he could change Katherine's mind. *We could have had a wonderful affair,* she'd said. Why had he been an idiot and not taken her up on it, then and there? He could have. Her kiss had all but invited him in.

But, of course, there was the twins to consider.

The package deal.

"I'm going to bed," he said abruptly.

"Good. Perfect place for you."

Gabe stopped in the doorway. "Dad? Why didn't you ever remarry?"

"Couldn't find a woman who would put up with the both of us." Gun hooked his finger through the cookie dough, popped a lump of it into his mouth and licked it clean, reminding Gabe of Andy and the ketchup. "Why? You wishing you had a mother to talk to tonight?"

Gabe opened his mouth to deny it, then shrugged. "Why would I wish for a mother, when I have such a fountain of information for a dad?"

Gun wiped his hands down the front of his Kiss the Chef or Get Out of the Kitchen apron. "I didn't remarry because I never found a woman I trusted enough to love you as much as I did. I thought if I was happy, you wouldn't be, and that I'd be sacrificing your happiness for my own."

"But what made you think I wouldn't have been just as happy…or even happier, if you had?"

Gun picked up the bottle of cinnamon and liberally spiced the cookie dough. "I always tell people that raising a kid is what made me a wise man, Junior. I never said it made me any smarter."

ON MONDAY MORNING, Gabe sat with his feet propped on his desk, shooting rubber bands at Santa Claus. It wasn't the *real* Santa, of course. Just a cardboard cutout decoration that Louisa put out on his desk every Christmas. So far, he'd knocked Saint Nick off the cardboard chimney three times. Three times out of thirty tries, which was not a great batting average.

He'd get better, though. Hell, there was still three whole days till Christmas.

The intercom buzzed, and he answered with a terse "Yeah."

"Your ten-o'clock appointment is here," Louisa's voice informed him.

Gabe deadeyed Santa and took aim. "I don't have a ten-o'clock appointment."

"You do now." Her tone brooked no argument. "And get your feet down off the desk."

His feet hit the floor with a guilty thud before it occurred to him that she couldn't have known where his feet were. She'd just made a lucky guess. Besides, last time he'd checked, he was still the boss.

But when Louisa opened his door a couple of minutes later, his feet were situated appropriately under his desk. He started to rise to greet a client, but sat again when he saw the red heads of Andy and Abby Harmon. Louisa didn't smile, just gave him a sharp be-nice-to-them nod before she stepped out of the room and closed the door.

Gabe clasped his hands on the desk and watched the twins watch him as if they'd never been in his office before, as if they were uncertain of their welcome.

"Come in," Gabe said, motioning to the chairs in front of his desk. "Does your mother know you're here?"

Andy and Abby exchanged a guilty glance before nodding in vigorous unison, which meant, of course, that if Katherine caught them down here, the aftermath would not be pretty. Gabe's hope that she had sent them ahead to break the ice died without ever taking a breath. "I suppose you're here to cancel our contract and get your money back?"

Abby's chin tilted alertly at that. "You're gonna give us money?"

Andy thumped her arm with his elbow. "We brought you a present," he said, keeping his hands behind his back as he and Abby advanced on the desk.

"A present," Abby concurred with a nod. "But you can give back our money, too. You were supposed to find Santa Claus and you didn't, so you can give the money back."

"Abby." Andy frowned severely at her. "You're not 'sposed to say that, 'member? We don't want to *fire* him."

She pouted a little. "I want my dollar back."

"We *want* the Christmas picture, Abby. Remember?"

"Oh." She wrinkled her nose and shifted from foot to the other, and it was all Gabe could do to sit still and not rush around the desk to hug them both. They wanted the Christmas in the picture. They still believed it was possible.

Satisfied he'd quelled the mutiny, Andy thrust forward a sack with the imprint of Santa's Workshop, North Pole, New York. "Me and Abby bought this for you yesterday. It's your Christmas present."

Gabe leaned forward and took the sack, wondering

if this was some kind of prank. But when he gingerly opened the sack, there was just a thick wad of tissue paper inside.

''We asked the lady at the gift shop to wrap it real careful so's it wouldn't get breaked.''

Abby nodded in perfect concurrence. ''It's a real special present, Gabe, so be careful with it.''

Inside the layers of tissue wrap was a cheap plastic snow globe, with a scene of a house set in a forest...well, not a forest, just three tiny trees, two tall and one small...but in front of the house was a miniature Santa with his sleigh and reindeer. Gabe shook the globe, and the snow scattered, swirling like magic around the little house in the picture.

''Thank you,'' he said, feeling inadequate and awkward and deeply touched by the gift and these kids. ''You didn't have to do this.''

''That's okay,'' Andy told him. ''Mom says if somebody gives you a present, you should give one back.''

Abby put her hands flat on the desk and lifted herself up until she could swing her feet from side to side. ''So, since we gave you a present, Gabe, you should give us one.''

He couldn't keep the tug of humor from dragging out his smile. ''Did you have something in particular in mind?''

Andy nodded, his eyes sparkling with new excitement. ''Me and Abby talked it over, and we want a lawyer.''

''A what?''

''A lawyer,'' Andy repeated, the *l* sound sloughing through the gap in his teeth.

"A lawyer." Gabe wanted to be sure he hadn't misunderstood. "Why do you want a lawyer?"

They looked at each other, then at him, and Andy lifted a skinny shoulder in an uncommunicative shrug.

Gabe tried again. "Do you know what a lawyer does?"

Abby sighed and stopped swinging. "He argues and goes to court to get stuff for people."

"So you want to hire a lawyer to go to court and argue and get your stuff, right?" Gabe tried to grasp the angle, but couldn't quite figure it out. "What do you want him to get for you?"

"Stuff," Andy said, looking at the desktop.

"Stuff," Gabe repeated. "Who has this…stuff?"

The twins looked at each other, then at him. "You do."

This was a nasty turn, Gabe thought. "Me? I have your stuff?"

They nodded, nearly in unison. "You've got Sparky and The Real Cat Matilda and we want 'em back."

Ah, the pets. "Look, kiddos, you don't have to get a lawyer and sue me to get your pets back. All you have to do is convince your mother to let you have them."

Again, they exchanged a glance, then turned their innocent, anxious blue eyes back to him. "We don't want the lawyer to argue with you."

The puzzle pieces fell into place. "I see. You want him to argue with your—"

"Mom." Together, they filled in the blank.

Gabe found himself faced with a twin dilemma.

On the one hand, he couldn't in good conscience encourage these kids to think it was all right to drag their mother into court over the custody of their pets. On the other hand, it might be the only way to keep Katherine from refusing a very special gift. Her past had left her scarred and distrustful of men and their commitments. His brief marriage had ruined a long-standing relationship and left him cynical about making any other commitments.

But right here, in his office, was the gift to heal them both. Abby and Andy, who didn't yet know that love and commitment were infinitely more difficult than turning an imaginary dog and a stuffed lion into warm, cuddly animals. Andy and Abby, who weren't afraid to believe they could have whatever they could imagine...a dog, a cat, a Christmas they could draw in crayon and wish into existence.

Gabe wanted to believe he could have the family he imagined, too. He wanted to believe that in twenty years he'd still be able to look across his desk into trusting eyes and say unequivocally, *"Yes, there is a Santa Claus."*

He made up his mind and punched the intercom. "Louisa? Get Max Costanza on the phone."

"What do you want with that publicity-mongering ambulance chaser?"

Gabe smiled. At last, he was going to get to tell Louisa something she didn't already know.

KATHERINE was pretty sure she was coming down with a cold. That was the only explanation for the draggy, achy feeling that had settled over her like a rain cloud. She'd gotten plenty of rest on Sunday, so she couldn't be tired. The twins had been relatively quiet, but then, she'd made them mad early in the day with a lecture on their behavior the day before. She'd half expected Gabe to pester her with calls or unannounced visits, but the phone had stayed silent, and the only one to knock on their door had been Raymond, wanting to see how the "new pet owners" were doing.

She already regretted that decision, but it was done. And it was the right decision. The twins weren't mature enough for the responsibility of a pet. And she certainly didn't need another living thing that depended on her for food, water, love, and well-being. She didn't even know why she still missed the kitten's fuzzy face and the dog's soothing presence.

But it was early in the week yet...only Monday and, although she'd had to come into the office for a few hours this morning, she'd made plans to take the twins to see *The Nutcracker* that afternoon. And tomorrow they were going to finish their shopping. And the day after, they'd put up the artificial tree. And then it would be Christmas Eve, and then Christmas Day, and by then they'd have forgotten all about Sparky and the kitten.

So would she. And she'd have forgotten all about Gabe, too. Forgetfulness was the only gift she was giving herself this Christmas...and if she knew where to buy it, she'd already have it in her possession.

Getting up from her desk, she walked out to the reception area to check on the twins. With her injured foot propped on a pillow, Janeen was reading short stories for the magazine's summer fiction bonanza issue, and she merely glanced up as Katherine entered. Abby and Andy glanced up, too, glanced at each other, then bent their heads over their sketchpads again so quickly, almost made her uneasy. Probably, though, they were just trying to follow her explicit and no-nonsense instructions to stay out of trouble. Which was a good thing. Really good, in fact. It had to be just her imagination that made her feel as if something not-so-good were afoot.

A half hour later, she was facing Max Costanza, a small platoon of reporters, and the information that her children were taking legal action against her to preserve their right to a champion schnauzer, a pedigreed cat, and the Christmas advertised in the December issue of *Contemporary Woman*. Oh, and just incidentally, Max added with barely concealed glee, the children felt it ought to be their right to believe in Santa Claus, even if she didn't.

The not-so-good something had a name...the Santa suit.

MAX COSTANZA was a man of short stature and tall ambitions. He had an eye for the prize and a profile heaven-made for the camera. But even though he had the glib tongue and quick wit to turn the twins' desire to believe in Santa Claus into a three-day media circus, Katherine couldn't figure out how he'd been able to convince Judge Robert Abernathy to grant a hearing on the matter. Even her attorney, Smitty Goldman, couldn't offer any better explanation than that the holidays were a slow time at the courthouse.

Still, Katherine was amazed to find herself sitting in a courtroom the following afternoon. She wasn't, however, in the least surprised when Gabe—who had been conspicuously absent and unavailable for questioning during the preceding twenty-four hours, slipped into a seat behind her in the courtroom and leaned forward to say, "Sorry, I couldn't be here sooner. I've been reading about it in the papers, though. How're you doing?"

She looked at him with eyes so cool it was a miracle he didn't freeze right there in his seat. "Oh, I'm fine," she said sarcastically. "I'm having a wonderful time."

His warm brown eyes just smiled blithely into her stormy grays. "You've certainly been getting a lot of publicity. I don't think there's a copy of *Contemporary Woman* left anywhere in the tristate area. That's one good thing, anyway."

One good thing. He had the audacity to say that to her... And when she saw the twins wave to him happily from their seats across the way from hers, she was ready to sue him for alienation of affection. Not that she really had a case against him—obviously her children didn't like her any less because they also liked him—but it was apparent that no one needed a case to file suit in this city. And if she had to sit through this mockery of a hearing on the custody of two animals and some legal clown's assertion that she was somehow preventing her children from having a satisfactory relationship with Santa Claus, then she could surely sue Gabe because she didn't like his annoying quirk of a smile.

Gun slipped into the seat next to Gabe, and when Katherine glanced coolly at him, too, he winked and gave her a thumbs-up. "Don't worry," he whispered. "Bob's a fair judge. I've known him for years."

Katherine turned an accusing gaze on Gabe. "The monthly poker game, I assume."

Gabe looked a little guilty. "Dad has never once beaten the judge."

"I have to let him win," Gun explained. "Never know when you may need a legal favor."

Katherine saw Gabe nudge Gun with a cautioning elbow, but as Judge Robert "Poker Face" Abernathy chose that moment to bang his gavel and quiet the hubbub in the courtroom, she let it slip past unchallenged.

Abby and Andy took the stand together, looking a little nervous, but determined to enjoy all the attention they were receiving. At home, they were subdued and well aware that they had not only stepped over the line of acceptable behavior, but had really hurt Katherine's feelings into the bargain. She'd made certain they knew exactly how she felt about their actions. She'd also made certain they understood how much she loved them and that she would forgive them. But she didn't tell them she laid the entire blame for this whole sordid episode at Gabe's door. He could look at her with those seductive eyes all he wanted. She wasn't forgiving him.

"We just want our dog, Sparky, to come home," Andy told the hushed courtroom toward the end of Max Costanza's melodramatic questioning.

"And The Real Cat Matilda," Abby added.

"And you want to believe in Santa Claus," Max prodded. "Isn't that right?"

The twins nodded in an alternating agreement.

"We'd like to believe he's real," Andy said. "Before we get too old to believe, like our mom did."

"Soooo..." Max drew out the word like an accusation, turning his body toward Katherine, his profile toward the camera. "Your mother doesn't believe in Santa Claus...and she won't let you believe in him, either. Is that correct?"

Next to Katherine, Smitty jumped to his feet. "Your Honor, my client has a perfect right to rear her children within the parameters of her own belief system. This court has no jurisdiction over the way she chooses to do that."

"Your Honor!" Max exclaimed. "She's denying these precious children a treasured piece of their childhood, the respect of their peers, the magic of Christmas, the—"

"Yes, yes, Max," Judge Abernathy said, interrupting him. "But let's get to the bottom line here. Miss Harmon?"

Katherine got to her feet. "Yes?"

"Can these kids have their pets back?"

She thought about arguing, but she simply wanted out of this courtroom, out of reach of the slow-news-day media mentality. "The pets can come home," she said. "Providing the person who gave them to Abby and Andy contracts a reputable, dependable pet-care service."

"Done." Judge Abernathy struck another blow with the gavel. "Anything else?"

Katherine began to feel better. "As a matter of fact, I do have something to say. There has been a great deal said about my unwillingness to let my children believe in Santa Claus. I would just like to point out that no one has said or done anything here to change my mind. But to show that I am fair-minded, I'll be perfectly happy to admit I was wrong and to let Andy and Abby believe in Santa Claus...if there is anyone in this courtroom who can prove he really does exist.''

The judge leaned to the side, zeroing in on Gabe and Gun. ''This would be the time for one of you heroes to jump in here and take the challenge.''

''Your Honor.'' Max protested the swing of attention away from his worthy self. ''I can't believe you're willing to let this matter disintegrate into a philosophical battle. It's perfectly obvious these children are—''

''Sit down, Max.'' The judge raised an expectant eyebrow at the Housley men, sitting behind Katherine. ''Is one of you going to volunteer? Or do I have to order you to do it?''

Behind her, Katherine heard the shuffle of feet as Gun stood up. ''I volunteer,'' he said gruffly. ''I volunteer my son to prove that Santa Claus really does exist.''

''Done.'' Judge Abernathy slammed down the gavel. ''This court is dismissed until tomorrow morning, nine o'clock.'' He looked at Gabe. ''Get your evidence together, son, because I will expect to leave here tomorrow believing there is a Santa Claus.''

The courtroom broke into calamitous activity. Abby and Andy looked around, as if they didn't know what they were supposed to do next. Smitty Goldman congratulated Katherine and himself on having this one ''in the bag.'' Katherine turned toward Gabe, the light of battle in her eyes. Gun tried to waylay Max, who was heading for the staging area and another news conference.

Gabe was the only person in the room who remained sitting, solemn, sober...and stunned.

"WAY TO GO, Dad." Gabe slammed the front door behind them. "Max and I spent hours planning our strategy, and you and the judge plotted for fifteen minutes this morning over a cup of coffee and managed to ruin everything."

"We saved your butt, Junior, and don't you forget it." Gun hung up his coat and cap and headed toward the kitchen. "All you have to do is go in there tomorrow, state your case, and voilà, Katherine forgives you, the kids get the dog, the cat, and Christmas, and you're a hero. Hell, your face will probably be on every magazine cover in the world."

"Oh, well, I never thought of it like that!" Gabe tossed his coat toward the coat tree in the hall, not caring that it missed and fell to the floor. "Katherine is never going to forgive me, Dad. Not now. She was all set never to speak to me again anyway, and now she gets to gloat while I make a complete ass of myself in front of the entire world."

"She won't *gloat*. She may enjoy watching, but she won't gloat."

"If Max had just been able to finish his case, we could have gotten her to agree to joint custody of the animals, which for all practical purposes would have given me joint custody of Abby and Andy, too, not to mention that Katherine would have had to talk to me."

Gun shook his head. "You remember telling me

the other night about how you felt like a comet, hurtling through the sky?''

Gabe nodded curtly. ''I remember.''

''Well, you burned up on entry. You're not thinking clearly, Junior. There's a simple solution here. And it doesn't involve Max Costanza or joint custody arrangements.'' He began clearing the counter. ''Now, I'm going to mix up another batch of cookies. Sugar cookies for Abby and Andy to decorate—and I suggest you quit acting like a moron, go over to Katherine's apartment, apologize profusely, then tell her you're so crazy sick in love with her you're not thinking straight and would she please just marry you and put you out of your misery.''

''Oh, now that's an easy solution,'' Gabe said, feeling finally defeated. ''Any chance I had with her got buried under all the headlines, and now I've got to *prove* there's a Santa Claus. Max assured me he can work miracles in a courtroom, but even he isn't willing to touch this...not even to get his face on all the magazine covers in the world.''

Gun set out the mixing bowl. ''You don't need a miracle, Junior. All you need is to believe in Santa Claus.''

''Oh, right,'' Gabe said with heavy sarcasm. ''Now, why didn't I think of that?''

''You're not a wise man, yet,'' Gun answered. ''But you will be. You will be.''

Chapter Twelve

The courtroom filled with hushed excitement as Gabe approached the bench. He was nervous. So nervous he could hardly breathe. He hoped he was right about this. For Abby's and Andy's sake, he hoped he was right. For his and Katherine's sake, he had to be.

He felt every eye in the place follow him as he placed the box he carried on a low table. But he pretended a confidence he was far from feeling as he took out the items and hung them, one by one, on a display stand he'd put in the courtroom earlier. The red velvet pants went on the hanger first, then the fur-trimmed jacket, around which he looped the black patent belt, with its big gold buckle. He looped a fake white beard over the hanger and placed a pair of shiny black boots on the floor. Then he topped the outfit off with a red velvet hat, complete with white trim on the brim and tassel.

"Judge Abernathy, Andy, Abby, Katherine, Mr. Goldman, ladies and gentlemen, this—" he indicated the display "—is a Santa suit. It's an empty costume, a bit of velvet and fake fur, a belt, a hat, and a pair of boots. Nothing special, just a funny-looking outfit that most of us would never have any occasion to wear.''

Turning again to the box, he took out his coat and hung it next to the costume. "This is my coat. It's my favorite coat and it happens to be a design by Armani. It's not the original, there are probably a couple of hundred just like it in this city alone. But it's my coat, and there are a number of people in this courtroom—'' he let his gaze drift to Katherine "—who could tell you it's mine. They recognize it, you see, because they've seen me wear it.''

He took a deep breath and focused on Katherine, closing out every other pair of eyes but hers, pushing aside the awareness that anyone else was watching. He didn't care if he convinced another soul with this performance. He wanted to sway her heart, and hers alone. "There are a few people who might try to tell you all the things they know about me just by looking at my coat. They might say I like dark, somber colors because the coat is brown. They might say I live in a cold climate because the coat is heavy and it's made of wool. Some people might say I'm generous, because the coat has deep pockets. Or that I'm stingy because those same pockets show no sign of wear. Every one of you is looking at my coat right now and thinking you know something about me, even if it's only that I have terrific…or terrible…fashion sense.

"But the truth is, it's just a coat. An empty coat. It doesn't really tell you a thing about the person who wears it. On the other hand, we all know a lot about the person who wears the Santa suit. We know he's kind, generous, jolly, and that he likes cookies and milk. We know he represents the best in all of us, the qualities we'd all like to believe are universal among the human race. We know that his is a spirit of joy and possibilities. We know that if there really isn't anyone who can fill these boots, the world would be a sad and dreary place. As dreary as a world without a single pair of twins, a world without red hair and freckles, a world without imagination or hope.

"I can't prove the existence of Santa Claus. I can't prove the existence of hope. Or love. Or imagination. But I can show you this—'' he picked up Abby's drawing and held it out to Katherine ''—and I can tell you that it represents the hopes, the dreams and the imaginations of two very wonderful kids. I can tell you that for the past five years I've been a skeptic about love and commitment. I thought that being responsible for a family was the very last thing I ever wanted to do. But then Abby and Andy walked into my office, and I committed to do the most foolish thing imaginable. I promised them I'd find the real Santa Claus, and prove to their mother that it wasn't too late to believe in magic.

"Well, I don't know if I could ever convince her of anything except that I'm the greatest jackass on the face of the earth. I only know that when I look at Abby and Andy, I believe in Santa Claus and the elves and that reindeer can fly one day a year and that an imaginary dog and a stuffed lion can become real. And when I look at you…'' He put his hands down on the table in front of Katherine and leaned toward her. "When I look at you, Kate, I believe in all the things I could never hope to prove. I believe in love at first sight and love forever after and love that comes in packages of three. And I'm willing, eager, to spend the rest of my life proving that to you.''

"Gabe..." she whispered, hers eyes shiny with unshed tears.

"I love you, Katherine," he said. "I love your children. I love your dog and your cat and your coffee. I know I'm asking a lot, but could you just once step out in faith and believe in something you can't see. Believe in me. Trust me. Love me. Marry me.''

"Marry you?" A tear slid free and rolled down her cheek. "For real?"

"I don't know any other way to make the drawing come true," he said. "It clearly calls for a mom, a dad, two kids, a dog, and a coat...*cat*. I meant to say cat.''

"I'm not marrying you without the coat. You'll have to wear it to the wedding.''

"I'll wear the Santa suit, if you want.''

"No, the coat will be fine."

He took her hand. "So you will? You really will?''

"I will," she said. "I really will.''

Then he pulled her out of the chair, into his arms, and kissed her before she had a chance to change her mind.

Around them, the courtroom broke into raucous and riotous applause, and Judge Abernathy pounded his gavel to be heard above the roar. "The Santa suit is hereby dismissed. And if interested parties will step into my chambers, we'll take care of the legalities before we all go home for Christmas!''

And that is what they did.

"DAD! Look what I got from Santa!" Andy held up the Jet Jupiter Space Station and Launch Kit. "This is so cool!"

"Dad! Look I got one, too!" Abby held up a duplicate. "And I got a Barbie Astronaut, too!"

"What's in that package?" Katherine pointed to a small, square box, and Abby dived under the tree to get it.

"This is from Santa to Gabe," Abby read from the tag. "It should say from Santa to Dad, though, 'cause he's not Gabe anymore, he's Dad."

"What about me?" Gun was sitting on the floor between the twins, surrounded by nearly enough discarded wrapping paper to cover him. "I'm Gabe's dad."

"No, you're Grandpop." Andy sent Jet Jupiter flying through the air, and it was caught by Sparky in an impressive leap. "Yay, Sparky! Good dog!"

"Has anybody seen The Real Cat Matilda?" Abby began tossing ribbons and paper, looking for the kitten.

"She's behind the tree, trying to get her paw into that paper chain," Katherine said, pointing to the place where the construction-paper decoration hung dangerously low to the floor. "Here." She thrust the small package Abby had handed to her into Gabe's hands. "Santa left this for you."

He rattled it, then tore off the wrapping and opened the box. "Buttons," he said. "In case I lose one off my coat."

"Or in case they all get ripped off...somehow," Katherine suggested with a saucy smile.

Gabe kissed her. "This is even better than the Christmas I got the pony."

"It was a dog," she said. "You asked for a pony, but you got a dog. See, I remember more about your Christmases than you do."

"Only because Dad talks too much."

"What's this?" Abby held up the most recently opened gift. "The tag said it was to me and Andy, but it's just the same old drawing."

"I think that was supposed to be mine." Katherine reached for the infamous drawing, the crayon Christmas that had started the whole thing. She looked at it fondly, her fingertip tracing the stick figures through the glass.

Gabe looked over her shoulder. "I amaze myself at times. Look around you. The kids asked for it, and I delivered."

Katherine pursed her lips skeptically. "You delivered, huh? Well, why don't you explain to me just exactly what you delivered."

"My pleasure, Mrs. Housley." He held up the picture and pointed first to the drawing and then to each counterpart in turn. "Well, they wanted a house," he began. "And here's the house."

"It isn't in the forest," she observed reasonably.

"No, but we do have a real Christmas tree, which we decorated ourselves."

"And it does have real presents under it."

"Yes, and there are some for you."

"Really? Can I open them?"

"Later. Now, pay attention, this is important. There's going to be a test."

"Mmmm." Clasping her hands behind her, she regarded the picture again with a saucy tilt to her head. "What's that?"

"I'll give you a hint. It isn't spaghetti."

She inhaled deeply. "Smells like turkey."

"That's because it is."

"And what's this?"

He looked at the blue stick figure. "That's me. The resemblance is quite extraordinary, you know."

"It is, isn't it?" Katherine frowned at the picture. "Oh, wait, I was looking at the turkey."

He took the picture away from her. "That does it. No presents for you...until you've kissed me."

She gave his a quick peck on the cheek. "Okay, bring on those presents. You know, I can't remember the last time I opened a present without knowing in advance what was inside. I may get to like this."

"You'd better, because I intend to shower you with surprises."

The twins shrieked as they discovered two five-dollar bills wrapped in clear plastic and labeled with their names. "Money!" Abby waved the gift through the air. "Mom, we got money."

"Wonderful." Katherine picked up the package Gabe had placed in her lap and turned it over in her hands.

"This is not your main present," he said a little self-consciously. "In fact, it's just something that reminded me of you."

She leaned forward to kiss him, her mood turning wistful and reflective. "You asked me once what I had against Santa and I told you some nonsensical thing about a pony."

"I remember," he said, taking her hand.

"Well, now I want to tell you the truth. A long time ago, when I believed in Santa Claus, I asked him for a present, and when I didn't get it that Christmas, I told myself I hadn't really wanted it anyway and I said I didn't believe anymore. I said I knew because of the gift I didn't receive that he didn't, couldn't exist. How could he deny something so small to a child who'd just lost her father? But he did and I knew he wasn't real."

He loved her with the soft caress of his hand at her temple. "What did you ask Santa to bring you?" he asked.

"It was nothing, really. Just something my dad said he would get for me and never did, something he said reminded him of me. So I asked Santa to get it for me. It was just a little ceramic angel with blond hair and a basket full of stars. But he said the thing about her that reminded him of me was that she was stretching out her hand, reaching for just one more star."

Gabe swallowed hard, knowing that somewhere out there, Santa Claus really was watching. "I think it's time you opened your presents, Kate."

"Now?"

"Now." He bent his head and kissed her tenderly, with all the passion of a kiss under the mistletoe and all the promise of a lifetime of Christmases to come.

A HOLIDAY RECIPE FROM THE KITCHEN OF
Karen Toller Whittenburg

This is a holiday favorite at my house. We make
the gingerbread men ahead of time and
spend a family evening decorating them.
Some of the cookies even hang on our
Christmas tree—if I manage to get to
them before my family eats them up!

GINGERBREAD MEN

3/4 cup shortening	2 tsp soda
1 cup sugar	1/4 tsp salt
1 egg	1 tsp cinnamon
1/4 cup molasses	3/4 tsp clove
2 cups flour	3/4 tsp ginger

Mix together the shortening, sugar, egg and
molasses. Add the remaining ingredients, mix
thoroughly and chill.

Roll a ball for the head, a larger ball for the body
and small snake rolls for the arms and legs. (Be
sure the snake rolls are not too much thinner than
the body, or they'll burn.) Use raisins to make a
face and buttons. Bake at 375°F for 6 minutes or
longer, depending upon the size and thickness of
your cookies. Cool thoroughly before icing.

REC708

162

From the bestselling author
of *Jury Duty*

Laura Van Wormer

It's New York City's most sought-after address—a prestigious boulevard resplendent with majestic mansions and impressive apartments. But hidden behind the beauty and perfection of this neighborhood, with its wealthy and famous residents, are the often destructive forces of lies and secrets, envy and undeniable temptations.

Step on to...

RIVERSIDE DRIVE

Available in January 1998—
where books are sold.

He's every woman's fantasy, but only one woman's dream come true.

For the first time Harlequin American Romance brings you THE ULTIMATE...in romance, pursuit and seduction—our most sumptuous series ever. Because wealth, looks and a bod are nothing without that one special woman.

THE ULTIMATE...

Pursuit

#711 ~~SHE'S~~ *They're* THE ONE! by Mindy Neff
January 1998

Stud

#715 HOUSE HUSBAND by Linda Cajio
February 1998

Seduction

#723 HER PRINCE CHARMING by Nikki Rivers
April 1998

Catch

#729 MASQUERADE by Mary Anne Wilson
June 1998

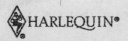

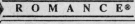

Once upon a time…

We were little girls dreaming of
handsome princes on white chargers…of
fairy godmothers…and of mountain castles
where we'd live happily ever after.

Now that we're all grown up,
Harlequin American Romance lets us
recapture those dreams in a miniseries
aimed at the little girl who still
lives on inside of us. Join us for stories
based on some of the world's best-loved
fairy tales in

Once Upon a Kiss…

Look for the next magical fairy-tale romance:

DADDY & THE MERMAID
by Charlotte Maclay
Available in January 1998

Once Upon a Kiss… At the heart of every
little girl's dream…and every woman's fantasy…

HFAIRY6

**Don't miss these Harlequin favorites
by some of our bestselling authors! Act now and
receive a discount by ordering two or more titles!**

HT#25720	A NIGHT TO REMEMBER	$3.50 U.S.	☐
	by Gina Wilkins	$3.99 CAN.	
HT#25722	CHANGE OF HEART	$5.50 U.S.	☐
	by Janice Kaiser	$3.99 CAN.	
HP#11797	A WOMAN OF PASSION	$3.50 U.S.	☐
	by Anne Mather	$3.99 CAN.	
HP#11863	ONE-MAN WOMAN	$3.50 U.S.	☐
	by Carole Mortimer	$3.99 CAN.	
HR#03356	BACHELOR'S FAMILY	$2.99 U.S.	☐
	by Jessica Steele	$3.50 CAN.	
HR#03441	RUNAWAY HONEYMOON	$3.25 U.S.	☐
	by Ruth Jean Dale	$3.75 CAN.	
HS#70715	BAREFOOT IN THE GRASS	$3.99 U.S.	☐
	by Judith Arnold	$4.50 CAN.	
HS#70729	ANOTHER MAN'S CHILD	$3.99 U.S.	☐
	by Tara Taylor Quinn	$4.50 CAN.	
HI#22361	LUCKY DEVIL	$3.75 U.S.	☐
	by Patricia Rosemoor	$4.25 CAN.	
HI#22379	PASSION IN THE FIRST DEGREE	$3.75 U.S.	☐
	by Carla Cassidy	$4.25 CAN.	
HAR#16638	LIKE FATHER, LIKE SON	$3.75 U.S.	☐
	by Mollie Molay	$4.25 CAN.	
HAR#16663	ADAM'S KISS	$3.75 U.S.	☐
	by Mindy Neff	$4.25 CAN.	
HH#28937	GABRIEL'S LADY	$4.99 U.S.	☐
	by Ana Seymour	$5.99 CAN.	
HH#28941	GIFT OF THE HEART	$4.99 U.S.	☐
	by Miranda Jarrett	$5.99 CAN.	

(limited quantities available on certain titles)

TOTAL AMOUNT	$ _____
DEDUCT: **10% DISCOUNT FOR 2+ BOOKS**	$ _____
POSTAGE & HANDLING	$ _____
($1.00 for one book, 50¢ for each additional)	
APPLICABLE TAXES*	$ _____
TOTAL PAYABLE	$ _____

(check or money order—please do not send cash)

To order, complete this form and send it, along with a check or money order for the total above, payable to Harlequin Books, to: **In the U.S.:** 3010 Walden Avenue, P.O. Box 9047, Buffalo, NY 14269-9047; **In Canada:** P.O. Box 613, Fort Erie, Ontario, L2A 5X3.

Name: _____
Address: _____ City: _____
State/Prov.: _____ Zip/Postal Code: _____

*New York residents remit applicable sales taxes.
Canadian residents remit applicable GST and provincial taxes.

Look us up on-line at: http://www.romance.net

HBKOD97